ALL CHANGE!

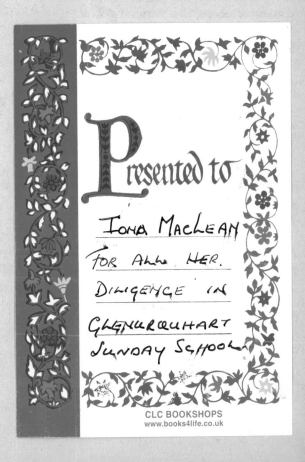

Presented to

Iona MacLean
for All her
Diligence in
Glenurquhart
Sunday School

Scripture Union, 207 209 Queensway, Bletchley,
Milton Keynes, MK2 2EB, England.

ISBN 1 85999 344 3

British Library Cataloguing-in-Publication Data.
A catalogue record of this book is available from the
British Library.

Printed and bound in Great Britain by
Cox & Wyman Ltd, Reading, Berkshire.

For Mum and Dad

Chapter 1

"I'm pregnant."

Whatever it was that I'd expected Mum to say, it certainly wasn't that. There had been some tension in the air around our house for several days, and tonight Mum and Dad had told us they had something they needed to talk to us about. In our family it's usually a bit ominous if the parents want us all to sit down and have a talk. I thought maybe Dad had lost his job, or that we were moving house or something.

"What did you say?" My brother Thomas had been leaning back on two legs of his chair and gazing at the ceiling. Now he bumped his chair back onto all four legs as he looked from Mum to Dad and then back to Mum again.

"I'm pregnant," Mum said again. She looked across at Dad who reached over the table and took her hand. "We're going to have another baby."

"Wow," I said. I probably should have congratulated them, but I was a bit lost for words. "When?"

"January, we think," Mum said. "We won't know for sure until they do a scan."

I tried to work out how many months pregnant she was; it was July now.

Dad must have seen me counting on my fingers.

"We think your mum's about three months pregnant," he said.

Thomas had been sitting there looking shocked. "Why didn't you tell us before?" he asked.

"We didn't know," Dad said. "You know Mum's been feeling sick recently, but we thought she was too old to have any more children. Anyway, when she fainted on Tuesday Dr Harris did some tests and told us this."

I couldn't believe it: Mum's older than a lot of my friends' parents, anyway. I suppose forty-five isn't exactly ancient... but a baby!

We all sat there without saying anything for a couple of minutes and then Dad launched into this speech about how they hadn't planned to have another child but that it was a very welcome surprise. He said it needn't change any of our plans about university or anything, and he hoped we would both be especially supportive to Mum from now on.

Thomas stood up. "I'm going out," he said abruptly.

"Sit down, I haven't finished," Dad said.

"I have," Thomas said, and then just walked out, slamming the front door behind him.

I looked at Dad questioningly as he made tight fists with both hands for a moment then slowly released them; I could see he was annoyed by Thomas' attitude, but trying to stay calm.

"Oh, go on then," he said, "I've said most of what I wanted to say."

It was weird going outside. Nothing seemed to have changed since I'd walked into the house an hour or so earlier on; it was still the same balmy July evening. The village still felt as sleepy as it always does. The only difference was that the shadows were starting to lengthen a bit now. That, and the fact that our family, which had always been a family of four, was now going to be a family of five. Mum's news seemed unbelievable really; I just couldn't get my head round it.

I felt a bit sorry for Thomas; he was obviously having even more trouble coping with the news than I was. I could see him up ahead of me, walking really fast down a track between the fields with his hands shoved down inside his pockets and his shoulders hunched. I broke into a run to catch him up. I don't often do that because I think with my long arms and legs it makes me look like an ungainly giraffe lolloping along. I tried explaining that to my PE teacher once, but he said I was talking absolute rubbish and there was no way I was getting out of athletics that easily.

Anyway, because I'm not used to running I was quite out of breath by the time I caught up with Thomas. I ran up and grabbed his shoulder. "What's the matter?" I panted.

"What do you mean, *what's the matter*?" he said, shaking me off. "Everything's the matter. Didn't you hear what Mum and Dad said just now?"

"That Mum's pregnant. So? I know it's all a bit of a shock but Dad says it doesn't have to change anything."

"Oh don't be so stupid, Hannah. Of course it changes things, it changes everything. They're not exactly going to be able to afford for me to spend five years at medical school now, are they? And our family isn't going to be just our family any more, is it? Plus, apart from anything else, Mum's too old to have a baby!"

"Forty-five isn't old," I said.

"It is when you're talking about having a baby," Thomas said. "She'll be an old-age pensioner by the time it's my age, and there's more things likely to go wrong during pregnancy and the birth."

I'd had enough. I hadn't had time to come to terms with the news myself yet; I could manage without Thomas' pessimism until I had. I left him to carry on walking by himself, while I cut down a footpath that led to a group of trees. It's a place we often used to go and play when we were younger. There's a massive old lime tree that's grown in such a way that it's got a sort of room in the middle, like a natural tree house.

I squeezed myself up through the little leafy tunnel into the tree. I know I'm too old for tree houses, but it's the only place I know to get any decent privacy. I sat with my knees pulled up to my chest, surrounded by the branches of the tree.

It was strange to think of Mum at home, probably making supper now as if everything was ordinary, but with everything different because a little baby was growing inside her.

In a way I was quite pleased. When I was little I always used to pray for Mum to have another baby when we were stirring the Christmas cake. It was like making a wish really and I did it every year until I was about ten, because Mum had once told me that Thomas had prayed for a baby while stirring the Christmas cake the year before I was born. I'd always wanted to have a little brother or sister, and now – when I'd finally given up hope – it was actually going to happen!

I sat there smiling to myself, listening to the breeze rustling the big green leaves of the old tree. Then I remembered Thomas' reaction. He was right, the baby was bound to change things an awful lot, and what about it being risky to have a baby at Mum's age? Thomas must have read that in one of his medical books. He's just finished the first year of his A levels, but he reckons the more he reads now the less he'll need to learn at medical school.

He's always wanted to be a doctor; it runs in our family. Gran and Gramps had a GP surgery in town until they retired and now my dad's sister, Aunty Joyce, is a partner there. Dad's not a doctor though; he's a landscape gardener. He says it's because – like me – he's not really academic, but we all know that really it's because he's too squeamish. He might be six foot three, but my dad even has to leave the room if they show an operation on *Pet Rescue*!

Dad loves his job, he says he likes being outdoors and sharing with God in the work of creation, but to be honest he doesn't make much money. Mum does some supply teaching to bring in a bit more, but our family's not exactly what you would call well off. That's why Thomas is worried that a baby will mean they can't afford to let him spend five or six years at university. Personally I didn't really think it would come to that. Gran and Gramps seem to be pretty loaded, and I couldn't see them letting Thomas pass up the chance to follow in the family footsteps.

After a while all my different thoughts and feelings about Mum and Dad having a new baby seemed to spin together and I just sat there, in the middle of the tree, looking at my feet resting on last year's dead leaves. I don't know how long it was before I realised it was almost completely dark and thought I'd better make a move.

I had just put my feet on the ground, after descending from the tree rear end first, when someone grabbed me from behind.

"Your mum told me what happened. I thought I might find you here."

"Karl! You scared me stupid!" I laughed. It was good to see him. Karl and I have been best mates since junior school, probably because we're the only people of our age in the village. I was glad I wasn't going to have to walk home across the dark fields on my own, and right now I really needed a friend to talk to.

"Did Mum tell you she's pregnant?" I asked him, brushing off some bits of dead leaves that had stuck to my backside.

"Yes," he nodded. "She said it wasn't public knowledge yet, but that she thought you'd tell me anyway."

"What did you say to her?"

"Congratulations! What else could I say?" He grinned at me. "What did *you* say? is more to the point. Your dad says you and Thomas didn't take the news very well."

"I did! It was Thomas that stormed out. He thinks it's going to change everything," I said.

"Isn't it?" Karl asked.

"I don't know," I shrugged. "Probably. I was just trying to get my head around it. It's sort of exciting and weird at the same time. I think it will take a while for it to sink in; it seems unreal at the moment."

Karl nodded; it was so dark now I could only just see him.

"I'm glad you came to find me," I told him, tucking my arm into his as we started to walk. "Did your concert go all right this evening?" As if it's not enough that Karl's clever, sporty and good-looking, he's also an incredibly talented musician. He plays the violin in the county orchestra. If he wasn't my best friend I think I'd probably find him either sickening or intimidating. Somehow, though, you don't see someone in the same way when you've learnt your alphabet together and seen them throw up on the reading rug at junior school. At least, I thought, even though my family is changing, I've always got Karl as my friend; nothing's going to change that.

Chapter 2

"What is it?" I asked. It was early morning and Mum was sitting at the kitchen table in her dressing gown, leafing through a pile of post. She'd just opened one of the letters and seemed to be particularly interested in what she was reading.

"It's from the antenatal clinic at the hospital," she said. "They want me to go for a scan and an appointment with the consultant. Blood tests as well." She raised her eyebrows. "Hmm," she said, turning to look up at me and smiling, "all of this certainly brings back some memories."

I was standing at the work surface, making cheese and pickle sandwiches. Karl and I had decided to go on a really long bike ride, and I'd managed to get landed with making the sarnies for our picnic lunch. Now I put down the knife that I had been using and went over to the table.

"When's the appointment for?" I asked, looking over Mum's shoulder.

"Tuesday 24th August," she read from the letter, "nearly two weeks' time."

"Oh," I said, "so Dad won't be able to go with you, will he?" Dad's work is usually pretty flexible, but that week he was going to be teaching a summer school on garden design at the technical college in town. He'd been getting really enthusiastic about it and preparing stuff for the lectures for ages. I doubted that he would let anything interfere with his plans now – not even the chance to see his new baby on a scan. Mum seemed to agree.

"Mmm," she said, "it is a bit of a shame he'll miss the scan. Mind you," she laughed, "it's probably for the best that he's not there if I'm having blood taken – you know what your dad's like with anything like that!"

She looked thoughtful for a moment. "I'm trying to remember if Dad came to any of my antenatal appointments when I was pregnant with you or Thomas," she said. "I don't think he did actually – but then again back then I don't think it was expected so much that men would."

Just then the doorbell rang.

"I could come to the appointment with you if you like," I said to Mum, in between licking pickle off my fingers on the way to answer the front door. "I don't mind watching them stick needles in you!"

It was Karl at the door. I'd hardly got it properly open when he practically threw his bicycle panniers at me, catching me just under the ribs and almost doubling me over.

"Feel the weight of those," he ordered me.

"Oof," I exclaimed, letting them slide to the floor, "What have you got in there? They weigh an absolute ton."

"Drinks," he said, "lots of them. If today turns out to be as hot as I think it will be, we're going to need them. Got any suncream?"

I nodded. "Yep, and you can carry that and the sandwiches, as well as this lot," I said, picking the panniers up and passing them back to him, "because no way am I cycling with that weight on the back of my bike."

"I wouldn't let you anyway," he said, grinning. Now *that*, I might add, is *not* because he's some kind of gallant bloke who won't let me carry stuff because I'm a girl. No, it's because these are his mega expensive panniers we're talking about. His parents actually made him save up to buy them for himself for once. Anyone who knows Karl's parents would know how unusual that is; he can usually persuade them to get him pretty much anything. I once heard Mum say to Dad that Karl is a spoilt only child. And it's true that he does have pretty much everything he wants – it makes him really hard to buy presents for. A couple of years ago I got him this really daft Christmas present: on the packaging it said "For the man that has everything – a real sheepskin belly button warmer" and inside there was just this tiny little circle of woolly stuff. Anyway, the fact that his parents wouldn't buy him these panniers just shows how totally over the top they are. Basically he spent a fortune just so that he could get the ones that were the same make as his rucksack.

I went round the side of the house and got my mountain bike out of the shed (well, it's Karl's old one actually – he managed to con his parents into getting him a new one with an aluminium frame), and we set off. It was still early and the air was quite cool – cool enough to give me goosebumps on my arms for the first half mile or so. The early cool didn't last long though and I was soon working up a sweat in the heat as I tried to match Karl's pace going uphill. As usual he just seemed to have an unlimited amount of energy. After we'd been going for a while the road took us through some woods and we stopped in the shade of the trees to have a drink. It was so nice to be able to sink to the ground and take my helmet off; it had felt tight on my forehead, making it all sweaty and horrible. But even while we were stopped Karl didn't relax; he was off climbing one of the big trees.

I watched him climb until it was hard to see him through the leaves. Where the branches were too far apart to step from one to another he swung himself up between them like some kind of monkey. It worries me a bit when he does stuff like that, but I know better than to say anything. He'd just make sure he climbed higher and faster if I did. After a couple of minutes I heard some rustling and looked up to see him making his way back down the tree.

"Show off," I said, as he jumped from the last branch and landed at my feet. He grinned, as if I'd meant that as a compliment. I stood up and dusted myself off. Karl was already back on his bike. I screwed the cap back on the bottle I'd been drinking from, and handed it back to him.

Karl was right, the day turned out to be a real scorcher. It just seemed to get hotter and hotter – one of those blazing August days that people seem to forget about when they complain about the British weather. I was glad that Karl had brought so many drinks. Especially as we weren't passing all that many places where we could buy them.

We'd planned our route so that apart from crossing a few main roads, it was mostly all along country lanes and through villages. Some of the roads we cycled along were unfenced and a couple of them were even gated. They really gave me a feeling of being out in the middle of nowhere, but basically we were just going in a big forty mile circle that took us right round the other side of town and back again.

On the gated roads Karl cycled ahead of me and opened the gates. When he'd closed them again he seemed to think he had something to prove by over-taking me again before the next one. When we reached one of the gates there was a flock of sheep in the way that were going to have to move out of the way before we could open it. It was so funny trying to shoo all these sheep away. Every time we'd just about man-aged it, a couple of them would dart around us and race back to the gate. They were making so much noise, baaing and bleating, that we were just about killing ourselves laughing. After a while we started to get a bit concerned that the farmer might come along and accuse us of sheep worrying or something. So in the end we just had to pick the bikes up and climb over the gate – I don't know what we would have done if we'd been in a car!

The hills that we were tackling seemed to be getting steeper as the day got hotter. In spite of my pride I had to get off and walk up one of them, pushing my bike. I could see Karl – already at the summit – consulting the map, and wished that I could've got there as effort-lessly as he seemed to have. Eventually though I did get to the top, and then there was just this incredible view spread out in front of us; you could see for absolutely miles and miles.

"Good, isn't it?" Karl said, watching me trying to catch my breath and take it all in at the same time. "On a clear day my dad says you can see right over to the Welsh mountains from here. Too hazy today, unfortunately," he said, passing me a bottle of water, which I took gratefully.

We got back on the bikes. I started off down the hill first, leaving Karl to fold the map up and put it away. I only needed to turn the pedals once and the gradient did the rest. It was one of those brilliant downhill runs that makes the uphill seem worthwhile – a long, straight stretch of road. Steep enough to go really fast, but not quite so steep that I needed to be braking all the time. The day was still, with no breeze, but as I raced downhill the rushing air cooled me and caught at the hair behind my helmet. Karl overtook me, head down for streamlining and T-shirt flapping madly behind him. I could hear him laughing crazily as he went past.

I wondered, suddenly, if Mum and Dad would let me do stuff like forty mile bike rides on my own or if my best friend was a girl. Somehow they always seem to think I'll be safe with Karl. They obviously don't realise how mad he can be sometimes, I thought, looking at him hurtling down the hill ahead of me.

Suddenly I found myself laughing too, exhilarated by the feeling of speed, and the wind in my face.

It was soon after that long downhill that I started to recognise the area that we were cycling through again, and realised that we must be on the final leg of the ride. Coming through one of the villages I remembered that it had a shop, so we turned off our route to buy ourselves some well deserved ice creams.

The shop was one of those little villagey places that has a sign saying "Post Office and General Store" outside; inside it was tiny. (A lot of the villages round our area are too small to have any shop at all – ours for one!)

As we went inside, the door jangled and I started to get the impression that I was in a time warp, and had just travelled back to the 1950s or something. They still had one of those big wooden counters in there, and loads of stuff stacked on wooden shelves that went up behind it, from the floor to the ceiling. It was quite cool and dark compared to outside but with that sort of musty smell that old buildings get.

Fortunately though, they were up to date enough to have a freezer stocked with our favourite ice creams – I reckon they probably get quite a bit of trade from the tourist boats that pass on the canal. I slid the perspex lid back from one side of the freezer and put my hand in to get the ice creams out. It was tempting to stick my head in as well, so as to cool off a bit, but a glance at the woman behind the counter changed my mind: I got the feeling she wouldn't be terribly impressed if I did.

We left our bikes propped up outside the shop and crossed the road to sit on the canal bridge to eat the ice-creams. I sat with one leg either side of the parapet, looking out across the countryside and watching the barges chug along the canal. Karl sat looking back at the shop, his eyes firmly fixed on his precious bike to make sure nobody made off with it.

I caught the gorgeous smell of cut grass on the air, and took a deep breath to savour it. I felt really peaceful sitting there, and I tried not to think about the miles we still had to cycle to get home. I idly let my eyes wander around, taking in the scenery.

There were horses grazing in the field closest to us, and beyond that cows lying lazily in the grass chewing the cud. I could feel the sun baking through the back of my T-shirt. It was so hot, now that we had stopped moving, that it actually made me shiver; weird. Birds I couldn't see were chattering in the trees by the canal. Suddenly a duck dashed out from under the trailing green branches of a willow, and hurried across the water, closely followed by three ducklings. They swam backwards and forwards along the other side of the canal for a bit, before choosing a place to scramble out onto the far bank with much splashing and quacking.

I turned to look at Karl. He wasn't looking at the ducks or anything, just watching the bikes and eating his ice cream.

I nudged him. "It's really beautiful, isn't it?" I said.

"What is?" he asked, pulling the wrapper down his ice cream and taking another bite, still without taking his eyes off the bikes.

"You know," I said, gesturing vaguely at the countryside, "creation and stuff."

"Hmm," he said, looking round briefly. "Yeah, I suppose so. But it's not 'creation' you know – you're forgetting I don't believe in all that rubbish."

"Oh, so what is it then?" I said, feeling a bit annoyed with him for spoiling my mellow moment. "You can't really think that all of this just somehow got here by accident, can you." I'm sure he knew it wasn't meant as a question, but he answered anyway.

"Yep," he said, "just one great big cosmic accident.

Big bang, then *whoom...* universe. Pure chance we're here at all," he said matter-of-factly, pushing the rest of his ice-cream into his mouth and screwing the wrapper up in his hand. I think sometimes he quite enjoys winding me up.

"Eat your ice cream before it turns to milkshake," he said. I knew he said that to end the conversation. Whenever we get onto anything at all religious first Karl winds me up and then he shuts me up. He says he's an atheist, that he has a positive belief that there is no God, and he won't discuss it any further with me. He says he wouldn't mind talking about it if I didn't take it all so personally. But how can I not take it personally when he says that God doesn't exist? I've been brought up to believe God is as real as my parents and that Jesus is a good friend – even better than Karl is.

"Did I tell you I'm planning to audition for the National Youth Orchestra?" Karl said, changing the subject. "Now that I've been promoted to first violins in the county orchestra I reckon I must be in with a reasonable chance."

I'm sure the last ten miles of the ride were longer than the others. My legs were aching, I was getting a numb bum from the bloke's saddle on the bike, and every push of the pedals was an effort. My knees had gone really stiff after resting on the bridge and were now threatening to give up on me completely. Not that I was going to admit any of this to Karl. I tried to pretend that I felt really fit and would have liked to have cycled much further. Actually Karl's pace seemed to have slowed down too, and we cycled side by side for the last few miles.

"What do you want to do tomorrow, then?" he asked. "Another day of the holidays awaits us, like a fresh white page with no school on it."

"Oh, *very* poetic," I said sarcastically. "How about doing a sixty-mile bike ride?"

"Yeah right," he said, "as if *you'd* be up for it after today. What about the open air pool? I could get in some serious laps while you do your girlie bit of sunbathing."

The open air pool in town is one of the best things about summer where we live. Both sets of parents had given us multi-swim tickets at the beginning of the holidays, so all we had to fork out for was the bus fare to and from town. Quite often we could even manage to cadge a lift off one of our mums. Unfortunately though I had to remind Karl that tomorrow was Friday.

"Not quite a holiday really," I said to him, "Not since your bright idea to get yourself the paper rounds for all the local papers!"

Usually I helped Karl to deliver the papers and we split the money between us. I didn't generally mind doing it unless it was really bad weather – even then it could be quite a laugh going round with Karl, dripping wet. It was quite a good idea really – it only meant delivering to our village and the next one (which is sort of joined on), but the money, from delivering three different papers at once, really added up.

Right now though, lugging all those papers around was the last thing I wanted to do; I was looking forward to a long cold drink from the kitchen tap followed by a deep bath. As for tomorrow, sitting on the grass by the open air pool and having the occasional dip and gentle swim seemed a much more attractive prospect than the paper round, but reluctantly we agreed it would be better to leave the pool until we could make a whole day of it.

As we came in on the road at the top of our village Karl suddenly turned to me.

"Come on," he challenged me, "I'll race you back to your house."

I didn't even have the energy to reply, I just watched him belt away while I rested my feet on the pedals and freewheeled slowly down the road.

Chapter 3

Mum and I had been sitting in the waiting room for about half an hour. Her antenatal appointment was for 2 pm and it was now twenty-six minutes past.

"It sounded like Dad's summer school went pretty well yesterday, didn't it?" I said, making conversation.

"Mmm," Mum said, seeming distracted. Mum's usually a very patient person but she was starting to fidget. She picked up a magazine and then put it down again without reading it, and glanced repeatedly towards the ladies toilets. I think the two pints of water they'd asked her to drink before the scan were giving her grief.

An obviously pregnant girl came out of a room off the waiting area and shuffled quickly into the toilets. A couple of minutes later a lady wearing a white uniform came out of the same room holding some notes.

"Yvonne French please," she called, keeping the door of the room open with one foot.

Mum and I stood up and followed her into the room.

"Hello, Mrs French, I'm Helen, could you just pop up on the couch for me please?"

"Hello," Mum said as she took her shoes off and eased herself up on to the couch. "This is my daughter, she's come to keep me company."

"Helen" gave me a curt nod – she obviously wasn't interested who I was – and started pulling at Mum's clothes to get at her tummy. Mum had thought carefully about what to wear and decided on leggings and a T-shirt, "So that they've got easy access to my arms and tummy for all the things they're going to do to me," she'd said.

It was weird to see Mum lying there with her tummy out, and although I was interested in the scan and stuff, I did feel a bit embarrassed.

Next Mum had some blue jelly squirted onto her tummy, then Helen put the ultrasound probe on it and moved it around a bit. She seemed to be pressing quite hard. A black and white image came up on the monitor attached to the machine, but I was disappointed not to be able to make out anything that resembled a baby. I wondered if Mum could somehow have got it all wrong. Maybe she wasn't pregnant after all. She certainly didn't have a bump like the girl that had been in the scan room before us.

I was surprised by how quickly the scan was over. Mum was handed a bit of blue paper to wipe her tummy with.

"Right then," Helen said, "everything seems to be fine. Do you want a picture of the baby?"

"Yes please," Mum said, sliding down off the couch, and I watched as Helen pressed a button on the machine and two pictures scrolled out. As we left the room Mum handed them to me to look after while she scurried off to the loo. So, out of all the family, it was me who saw the baby first.

I sat down in the waiting room and turned the pictures around trying to make them out. Suddenly I could see the baby in first one and then the other. When Mum came back from the ladies I pointed it out to her enthusiastically.

"Look, it's lying on its back in this one – that's its little arm, and I think those are its feet. And look, there's its little nose!"

"Oh isn't it sweet?" Mum said, taking the pictures from me so that she could have a better look. "I had an ultrasound when I was pregnant with you," she said, "but they didn't give me a picture."

"It's amazing, isn't it?" I said. "I mean, it looks so human already, and you've hardly even got a bump yet."

We didn't have long to wait before Mum was called into another room by the midwife, who introduced herself as "Claire". She weighed Mum, and did stuff like taking her blood pressure. Each time she did something she explained to us what she was doing and why. Then she said she wanted to listen to the baby's heart. She explained that she was going to use a "Doppler" to pick up the heartbeat, and that it worked in much the same way as the ultrasound scan that Mum had just had. She put some more jelly on Mum's tummy and again a probe was pushed around. Suddenly she stopped moving the probe and looked up at us, smiling. I realised the "da-dum, da-dum, da-dum, da-dum" sound that the Doppler was making must be the baby's heart beating.

After that Claire used a needle to take two little tubes of blood out of one of Mum's arms. She explained what they would be testing it for, and checked with Mum to see if there were any tests she'd rather not have. Mum said no, it was fine to go ahead with all of them.

Claire also asked Mum if she'd had any thoughts about her "birth plan" yet, and gave her a big book and a load of leaflets to read when she got home. She explained that she would be Mum's "named midwife" and would try to see her at most of her antenatal visits. She said that, if possible, she would also be there for the birth, but that would depend on her shifts and when the baby chose to put in an appearance.

"Most of the time you'll see me rather than the doctor," Claire said. "You're going to see the consultant today because your age puts you in a higher risk category. If you want to see a doctor at any other stage that can also be arranged, but all being well we would expect that it would be me or one of the other midwives who will deliver the baby for you."

Then it was back to the waiting room again, before Mum was called in to see the doctor: "Mr Wallace – Obstetric Consultant" it said on the door.

"What does that mean?" I asked Mum, pointing at the door.

"What? Obstetric Consultant?" she said, standing up. "It just means he's a doctor who helps people to have babies."

Mr Wallace ushered us in and asked us to have a seat, so Mum and I sat down on two polished wood upright chairs. The other rooms we had been in had just had functional modern furniture and hospital equipment in them, but Mr Wallace's room was quite different. He walked round his leather-topped wooden desk and sat down in a big swivel chair on the far side. There were two bookcases full of variously sized books, some arranged neatly, some all higgledy-piggledy. There was also a very healthy looking cheese plant in a brass pot.

I wondered if it was real or artificial – it looked a bit too perfect somehow. But apart from the over-perfect plant, the room was not unlike Aunty Joyce's consulting room at Gran and Gramps' old surgery.

Mr Wallace had opened Mum's notes, and was having a quick read.

"I see you're forty-five," he said, in a refined but noticeably Scottish accent. "When was your last pregnancy?"

"Fourteen years ago," Mum said, nodding at me, "with Hannah."

The doctor looked at me over his half moon glasses for a few seconds.

"Well," he said at last, "I would not have thought you were only fourteen years old, young lady."

He had said it kindly, but I was glad when he turned back to Mum because I could feel my cheeks going hot as the blood rushed to my face. I don't know why what he said made me blush. I should be used to comments like that because I've always been very tall for my age. Last time I was measured I was 5'10", and people have always assumed that I'm older than I actually am. I suppose I just take after Dad; Thomas is tall too, but then so are most of his friends.

I switched my attention back to what Mr Wallace was saying to Mum.

"...so we'll be wanting to keep a special eye on this pregnancy," I heard him say in his gentle accent, "in view of your age, you understand."

I was lying on the grass by the open air pool. Karl was timing himself swimming lengths.

I was thinking about what the doctor had said to

Mum about the risks associated with having a baby at her age. I hugged my knees and reassured myself it was still quite unlikely that anything would go wrong for Mum or the baby.

I hadn't noticed Karl swim over to the side of the pool.

"What are you thinking about then?" he demanded, wet chin resting on his wet arms, folded on the concrete edge of the pool.

"Mmm?" I said. "Oh, nothing much really. Just about stuff they were saying at the hospital yesterday. Things the doctor and the midwife were talking about." I told him about them both saying Mum was "higher risk" because of her age. Then I found myself warming to the subject and enthusiastically recounted to Karl all the different things the midwife had done, like taking the blood and listening to the baby's heart. On the bus I'd already told Karl about seeing the baby on the scan, and was going to show him the pictures when we got home. Now I told him how surprised I'd been by all the stuff the midwives were able to do without having to refer to the doctors. The night before (after going to the hospital), I'd looked up – in Mum's big book – about the "birth plan" Claire had mentioned. It said it was about the midwives working in partnership with the pregnant woman to achieve the sort of birth she wanted. It all seemed really interesting.

"Sounds like you should think about becoming a midwife then, if it's all so fascinating," Karl joked.

"You know," I said, "that just might not be such a bad idea."

I shivered. The sun had gone in and big black clouds seemed to have appeared from nowhere.

"You going to give me a hand out, then?" Karl said, stretching one arm out towards me.

"Yeah, all right," I said, levering myself up off the grass, and walking the few steps over to the pool to drag him out.

In a split second I was under the water, disorientated and with strange muffled swimming pool noises in my ears. I came up spluttering for air and rounded on Karl.

"You rat!" I said. "You did that deliberately, and I'd just got dry in the sun!" I shook my head and pushed the wet hair back out of my face.

"That's me," he said, grinning, "your friendly water rat!"

I turned on him before he could get away, using one leg to push his legs out from under him and pushing his head under the water. Straight away the whistle blew and a lifeguard was pointing at me and telling me off. I was quite glad actually, because over the last couple of years Karl's definitely become physically stronger than me. When we're messing about you can pretty much guarantee he's going to win every time now.

It began to rain: big fat drops falling on the water. People started getting out of the pool, and those that had been sunbathing gathered up their things and scurried off to the changing rooms. I don't understand why people don't want to swim in the rain – it's not as if you're going to get any wetter, is it? Soon though it was just us left, and a couple of lads larking around at the deep end.

We swam around for a while, enjoying having the water pretty much to ourselves, then realised that this was the perfect opportunity for using the big water slide. It's like the flumes you get at leisure pools, but open to the air and not quite so steep. Usually there's a long queue to use it, so we don't bother very often. But now there was nobody waiting. We took turns to go down – sitting, lying, backwards, forwards – any way that wasn't going to get us into grief with the lifeguards, until we were getting too cold to keep climbing back up the metal stairs to get on it, and went back to swimming around in the relatively warm water.

The rain got harder, flattening the surface of the pool apart from little splashes as the drops hit the water. I could make out the lifeguards, in dripping wet T-shirts, consulting with one another as the heavy rain reduced visibility across the pool.

Suddenly there was a flash of lightning, closely followed by an almighty clap of thunder. The whistle blew.

"OK, everybody out!" a lifeguard shouted above the noise of the rain. "C'mon, I said *everybody out of the water*!"

As we swam for the side there was another flash of lightning and another clap of thunder, almost overhead this time. One of the lifeguards practically dragged us out as we reached the edge, then herded us into the changing block, locking a gate between us and the pool.

We sat quietly on the bus going home. The thunderstorm had passed over but it was still raining, and the windows were steamed up. The air inside the bus was hot, damp, and far from fresh, so that I felt slightly short of breath. I wished the driver would leave the door open to let some fresh air in.

"Pity we had to get out of the pool so soon," I said to Karl, "we could have had another couple of hours there if it wasn't for the stupid storm."

"Yeah, I suppose," he said, "but it was a good laugh while it lasted, wasn't it?"

He turned back to the window and rubbed it with his sleeve to see out. "When's your mum getting the results of those tests they did, then?"

"Not sure," I said, "in a couple of weeks' time maybe. But they said they wouldn't contact her unless there was anything out of the ordinary. So she probably won't hear until her next appointment."

A week later the hospital phoned. It was Mr Wallace's secretary. She asked Mum and Dad to go in to discuss the test results with him. I remembered the midwife saying that *all being well* Mum probably wouldn't need to see the doctor again. Mum and Dad kept saying that they were sure it was nothing to worry about, but privately Thomas assured me that it probably was.

I kept thinking of Mum and Dad while they were at the hospital. I imagined them sitting in Mr Wallace's office, with the perfect cheese plant, and I wondered what that gentle Scottish voice might be saying to them.

Thomas and I were both in the kitchen when Mum and Dad got back. I was getting a drink and Thomas was making some disgusting concoction involving peanut butter, marmite and cheese on toast.

I could see as soon as they came in that Mum had been crying, though she had now stopped.

"Hannah, Thomas," Dad said, "I'd like you to sit down, please. Your mum and I have got something we need to talk to you about."

The four of us sat around the kitchen table, just like we had the day Mum told us she was pregnant. Mum sat looking down at her clasped hands, which were resting on the tabletop.

"There's no easy way to say this," Dad started. "They told us at the hospital that Mum's test results indicate a very high risk that the baby may be handicapped."

"You mean the alpha-fetoprotein test?" said Thomas, who'd obviously been reading up on it. You can always rely on Thomas to start using technical terms.

"That's one of the tests that was mentioned, yes," Dad said, "but some of the other blood tests, as well as your mum's age, also indicate that the baby may well have Down's syndrome. Your mum and I have been talking about it on the way home, and it's not the end of the world. We both know people who have Down's syndrome, and they can bring special blessings to those around them.

"However," he continued, "the hospital has advised us to have another test: an amniocentesis. In fact they rather assumed that we would be having one, because then we would know for sure what the situation is."

"What's one of them, then?" I asked.

"An amniocentesis?" Dad said. "It means passing a needle into the womb to take a sample of the fluid around the baby, and from that, as I say, they can find out for sure whether the baby's handicapped or not. But your mum and I are concerned that the amnio carries a small risk of miscarriage. That is to say, it could cause your mum to lose the baby."

I heard Mum sob, just once, as she continued to look down without saying anything. I'm not used to seeing her get so emotional, and I felt a bit embarrassed by it.

"Why are you telling us all this?" Thomas asked Dad. "I mean, really it's your decision, isn't it – yours and Mum's?"

Dad looked thoughtful for a moment and then told us that he and Mum felt we must come to a decision about the test as a family. He pointed out that if Mum gave birth to a handicapped child, Thomas and I might well be left caring for our brother or sister after he and Mum died.

I covered my ears – I know it's a childish thing to do – but I couldn't bear it, all this talk about the baby being handicapped and Mum and Dad dying! I still heard what Thomas said next though.

"So what are you saying?" he demanded, "that you would consider an abortion if the baby's not perfect? Because that's the next logical step, isn't it? If the amnio is positive they would offer you an abortion."

I took my hands away from my ears and looked up, horrified.

"But you don't believe in abortion," I said to Mum, bemused, "and we've seen the baby on the scan... doesn't that make you feel anything for it?" I suppose it was a bit cruel to say that really, when Mum was already so upset. She looked up at this point. She looked at me, then at Thomas, and finally her eyes locked on Dad's for a few moments before she answered me.

"No, we don't believe in abortion," she said gently, "but because of what your dad has already explained we do feel that it's important for the whole family to be involved in making the decision."

"That's right," Dad said, "and at the moment the decision is simply whether or not we should have an amniocentesis done."

"No point then, is there?" Thomas said. "I mean there's no point risking the pregnancy to have a test done, if the results aren't going to affect what you do next."

We all agreed that he was right, but I saw Mum looking a bit uncertain, and I wondered if she would have preferred to have had the test anyway. Perhaps she would've liked time to prepare if she's expecting a baby with special needs, I thought. But I didn't say anything, because I didn't want Mum to risk having a miscarriage.

I lay awake in bed that night, thinking about all that had been said. I could hear Mum and Dad talking softly in the next room. It seemed strange that we would now have to wait months to find out whether or not the baby was handicapped. I tried to think about what Dad had said, about how Thomas and I might have to care for our brother or sister, but I couldn't imagine it, and even if it was going to happen it all just seemed so far in the future.

I tossed and turned for ages, wondering whether I should have said that I thought Mum would really have liked to have the test. I still felt that we had probably come to the right decision, although I thought it might be hard, waiting for all those months for the baby to be born, without knowing. I wondered if part of the midwife's job was to help people decide what to do in situations like this.

I still couldn't sleep. Finally, I got around to praying.

"Dear God," I said, "please let my little brother or sister be healthy and not handicapped at all. If that's not possible then please help us to love him or her just as much anyway. And please help me to understand what Dad meant about..." and then I must have fallen asleep, because I don't remember saying anything else.

Chapter 4

It was strange going back to school. So much seemed to have changed since we'd broken up for the summer holidays. It was hard to believe that we were in Year 10 now: the Year 10s had always seemed so old before.

Actually our year are looking pretty grown-up now. I've always been the tallest in the year, but now quite a lot of the boys have suddenly overtaken me. It was quite a shock when I realised that one of the ones who's suddenly taller than me is Karl – seeing him practically every day I hadn't noticed.

The best thing about that first day of term was catching up with the friends I hadn't seen over the holidays: Kirsty, Charlotte, Nicola – we all had loads to tell each other. Charlotte had spent the first half of the holidays doing loads of gymkhanas and showjumping. She said she was really annoyed that some people's horses had got "strangles" (apparently it's some kind of lethal horse disease), and so the Pony Club had cancelled all the events scheduled for the second half of the holidays. Nicola seemed to have spent the holidays much the same way I had: I don't think she had been away or anything. Kirsty had been to stay with her gran in Scotland. I get on all right with quite a few people at school, but Karl's the only person I'm really close to, and the only friend I usually see outside school. I don't know why I don't meet up with the others. I suppose it's just the hassle of it because they all live in town or the other villages.

Anyway, it seems that I might have to get to know my other friends a bit better, because the big shock of the first day back was that Karl isn't in any of my classes any more, except tutor group. Up to Year 9 we had all our classes with our tutor group, but now we're all on different timetables, depending on which options we took. Karl chose music where I chose art so he's in the opposite half of the year. It's strange, because ever since we started school the only time I've ever had a class without Karl is when he's been off sick or something.

Another thing I've got to get used to is that all our classes are 'streamed' now, according to our Year 9 test results. Amazingly I seem to be in most of the top sets, probably because last year Karl was forever explaining things I didn't understand to me! I wonder how I'm going to get on now that I haven't got him to help me in lessons – I'm not stupid, but like Dad I'm not exactly an academic either.

I started to feel a bit overwhelmed actually. All day long it just seemed to be one teacher after another telling us how much work we're going to have to do during the two-year GCSE course, and all the books we're going to need. Kirsty and Charlotte are still in most of my classes and when we bumped into Nicola in the corridor the four of us had a good moan about it all.

Although I spent a lot of the first day back at school

talking to people, I didn't tell anyone that Mum's expecting a baby. Somehow it didn't seem to fit into the "so what did you do in the holidays?" conversations. And also Mum's teaching at our school this term – ironically she's covering maternity leave for one of the English teachers! I'm relieved that she isn't teaching any Year 10 classes – I would have found that so embarrassing. Anyway, I thought it was probably better if the other staff heard about her pregnancy from her. But I think another reason I didn't say anything is because I don't really know how to react when people start saying congratulations now.

My whole family still seems to be pretty stunned by the news that the baby might be handicapped, although we haven't talked about it much. I think Mum and Dad find it hard to admit that they'd rather the baby didn't have Down's syndrome – they're so into loving everyone regardless. The way I see it, though, it's just wanting what's best for the baby. And I don't really think anyone would *choose* to have Down's syndrome.

I overheard Mum talking to one of her friends about the possibility that the baby might be handicapped. She said she felt quite at peace about it all, and mentioned the "special blessings" that Dad had talked about. But at other times I noticed that her eyes were red, and some mornings she didn't look as if she'd slept too well.

Wednesday was our third day back at school, and somehow everyone seemed to have worked out that a) Mrs French the English supply teacher was my mum, and that b) Mrs French the English supply teacher was pregnant. I don't suppose either was very difficult to figure out – a lot of people from the villages round our way know my mum and dad anyway, and Mum has at last started to get a bit of a bump.

People kept coming up to me in the corridor and asking if it was true that my mum was pregnant. I don't know exactly why the whole school seems to be so fascinated, but it was the same when one of the Year 11 girls was expecting a baby last year (she's left school now and has a little girl).

I don't really mind people being interested, nosy even, but quite a horrible thing happened when I was on the school bus waiting to go home. I was sitting on my own, waiting for Karl. I could hear the lads at the back of the bus laughing and whispering and I thought I heard my name mentioned. I tried to tell myself I was just being paranoid. Then a couple of minutes later one of the lads – Mark – walked slowly down the bus towards the front. I've never really liked Mark, he's too full of himself and always trying to make other people look stupid. I was relieved when he walked straight past me, but then he suddenly stopped and turned round. Very slowly and deliberately he put his hands on the seatbacks on either side of the aisle and then just started to stare at me with a sort of half smirk on his face. He carried on staring for what seemed like ages and I could feel myself going bright red, even though I was trying to pretend I hadn't noticed him. Then he turned to the bus in general, which was quite full by this stage, and everyone seemed to go quiet as he started speaking.

"Has everyone heard what Mr and Mrs French have been up to?" he said. I found myself twisting one of the straps on my bag around my hand, trying to ignore him.

"Yeah," one of the lads at the back shouted, "MAK-ING BABIES!" I heard several people around me sniggering. Looking down at my hands I saw that a couple of my fingers had gone blue because I'd twisted the strap so tightly around them.

"That's right," Mark said, his smirk now complete, "*making babies,* Hannah's mum and dad."

I was relieved to spot Karl getting onto the bus while Mark was speaking. I shifted myself over to the window seat to make room for him.

Karl pushed Mark out of the way.

"Shut up, loser," he said, and sat down in the seat next to me. But it didn't make a lot of difference.

"What's this got to do with you, Romeo?" Mark snarled at him. I was surprised to see colour rising on Karl's neck. He doesn't usually let the lads get to him.

"I was just going to say," Mark went on, "that I would like to offer Hannah here some friendly advice. Hannah dear," he said, leaning over Karl and putting his hand on my shoulder. He carried on despite Karl removing his hand with a white knuckle grip. "I think you should have a little talk with your mummy and daddy, explain the facts of life to them and tell them that they're getting a bit old for that sort of hanky panky. Maybe you should offer them some advice on contraception if you feel they're not getting the message; but then again it's a bit late for that, isn't it?"

All the lads at the back were practically in hysterics by this time. Mark was definitely getting the reaction he wanted from them.

Just when I was wondering if I could take any more, Mark suddenly seemed to lose interest. He shook Karl's hand off his wrist and wandered back up the aisle to his mates – probably because Thomas had just come out of the sixth form block and was getting on the bus.

But for some reason what Mark had said really upset me. It's not that that sort of thing is particularly unusual: I'm used to the stupid name-calling on the school bus (it's usually witty remarks such as "lanky long legs" and "Eiffel Tower" that are aimed at me). But somehow what they'd said about my parents and the baby really got to me. I must admit that I had been trying not to think about how the baby had happened in the first place, but it wasn't just that. I think it was the way they reduced the baby, this little miracle that I'd seen in the ultrasound pictures and heard on the Doppler, to the level of a dirty joke.

It wasn't long before I heard the baby's heart on the Doppler again. Claire had come round to the house to do one of Mum's antenatal visits. They were in the living room and Dad was with Mum this time. I was doing homework on the kitchen table, but I heard the "da-dum, da-dum, da-dum" noise of the baby's heartbeat coming faintly from the next room. I was also eavesdropping a bit, listening to all the stuff they were talking about. I heard Claire ask Mum about the birth plan again.

"Yes," Mum said, "I've been giving that a lot of thought actually. Tony and I have discussed it and we've decided we would like to have our baby at home."

There was a pause when nobody said anything. I put my pen down. Then Claire spoke. "Oh dear," she said. Then I heard her explaining to Mum and Dad that if they did have a home birth the midwives were legally obliged to support them in that choice.

"But I really don't think that a home birth is the best choice in your situation," she said. She went on to discuss complications which could be increased by Mum's age, and the medical treatments which might be necessary. She also said that the baby could potentially have certain problems which might require immediate resuscitation if it had Down's syndrome.

"Yes," I heard Dad's voice, "we know all that, and it's certainly not a decision that we've taken lightly. But everything was straightforward when our other two children were born and we've been told that this baby's heart and other organs are OK."

"Yes, well, as I say," Claire said, "if a home birth is what you choose I will support you in that decision, but I must make sure that you have all the facts and know the risks. And I do believe that in your particular circumstances a hospital delivery would be the best option, however nice a home birth would be if all went well."

"We've already made our decision," Mum said quietly. "Tony hates hospitals, and we want to welcome our baby into a loving home environment – especially if he or she does turn out to be handicapped."

All this home birth stuff was a new one on me: Mum and Dad hadn't said anything about it. I wondered if it might mean I'd be allowed to see the birth. But then again I wasn't at all sure if I'd want to.

Anyway, that evening Mum and Dad told us about their plan to have the baby at home. As it turned out, having all the family sitting round goggling at the birth wasn't quite what they had in mind. Basically they want Thomas and me to keep out of the way as much as possible; Dad said it would be a good idea for us to go round to friends' houses if Mum goes into labour during the day. That got me thinking: I'm starting to wonder if, after all the books and stuff we've been reading about it, this birth business could just turn out to be one big anticlimax as far as Thomas and I are concerned!

Chapter 5

"I can't believe it's nearly Christmas already," I said.

Thomas and I were sitting watching TV. The curtains were drawn against the wet night outside, and Dad had lit the open fire. Now he had taken a cup of tea upstairs to Mum who was resting on the bed to stop her ankles swelling. We were taking the opportunity to watch *Robot Wars*, which Mum hates and always tells us to switch off.

"You do realise that this will be the last Christmas that it's just the four of us, don't you?" Thomas said, without looking up from the TV, where one of the contestant robots was being beaten up by Sir Killalot. "Nothing will ever be the same again once this squalling brat of a baby arrives."

"Don't call it that!" I said, chucking a cushion at him which made him miss seeing the contestant robot being toppled into a pit by the house robot. He grabbed the cushion to retaliate, got up from the sofa and advanced menacingly towards the chair where I was sitting. I cowered down, trying to shield myself from the blows as he beat me over the head with the cushion, but I was laughing at the same time.

"Mercy! Mercy!" I shouted, trying to kick him without success.

The door from the hall opened and Dad came in. Thomas retreated back to the sofa and Dad picked up the TV remote. He turned the volume down and changed the channel over to the news.

"I really don't see how your mum is supposed to rest with the racket you two have been making," he said. "I'd have thought you were both old enough to show a little more consideration."

"Thomas called the baby a squalling brat," I said, deciding he deserved to be grassed up. "I was telling him to shut up, and he just attacked me."

"Yes, well, I daresay the baby will do his or her share of crying," Dad said mildly, but he looked tired. "You two certainly did."

Thomas was gesturing at me silently, indicating that he was going to kill me later.

The size of Mum's bump had been increasing steadily, so it was hard to ignore the fact that, as Thomas had said, soon nothing was ever going to be the same again. Soon the four Frenches would be five Frenches. But unlike Thomas I was really looking forward to the baby arriving. As Mum's size was increasing so was my excitement!

One day after school I had been to another antenatal appointment with Mum, just a routine check with the midwife. I was amazed by how much Claire could find out about the baby just by feeling Mum's tummy, or rather "palpating" as she called it. She said that the baby was still breech – sitting upright – but told Mum not to worry, as it would probably turn head down soon. She said that she thought the baby felt a normal size, and that it was facing forwards, which was probably one of the reasons why Mum was getting some backache.

When it was time to listen to the heart, Claire asked Mum if it would be all right to let me operate the Doppler. "Of course," Mum said, and smiled at me.

I squirted the jelly clumsily onto Mum's tummy and took the Doppler from Claire. She showed me the button I needed to press to make it work, and told me where on Mum's bump I was likely to pick up the clearest sound.

"You have to make sure that it's the baby's heartbeat that you're hearing rather than the mother's," Claire said. "The way to tell is that the baby's heart should be quite a lot faster, and you can check that you're listening to the right one by feeling Mum's pulse."

I managed to pick up the "da-dum, da-dum, da-dum" sound quite easily, and carefully held the probe in place on Mum's bump while I reached for her wrist with my other hand. Yes, there was no doubt about it, that was definitely the baby's heartbeat I'd located. I grinned: excellent!

After that Claire checked Mum's blood pressure and dipped a stick in the urine sample Mum had brought to the appointment with her. She asked Mum if it would be all right to take a blood sample, as she wanted to check that she wasn't getting anaemic. She explained that some women need iron tablets when they're pregnant. I plucked up courage and asked her how you go about becoming a midwife. She and Mum exchanged a quick knowing sort of a look and then Claire told me loads of stuff about different ways to train as a midwife. Apparently you can either train as a nurse first and then do another eighteen months or so training, or you can just train as a midwife straight away. She said that there were different courses available in different places and that you could even do a degree in Midwifery at the same time as the training if you wanted to.

"If you're interested I'll get some information and give it to your mum next time I see her," Claire said.

I nodded.

"Although I am only fourteen," I said.

"Never too early to start checking things out," Claire said. "You'll find some of the courses get booked up a long way ahead."

On the way home in the car I talked to Mum about the possibility of training as a midwife.

"I don't know why I haven't thought of it before," I said enthusiastically, "it's so much the sort of thing I'd like to do. I mean, I've got all the medical stuff in my blood from Gran and Gramps, but I've always known that I want to do something more practical, like Dad. And all the stuff Claire does looks so interesting. I'd really like to do all that. And then there's the babies – I really like babies!"

I was chattering away – it's not really like me to go on like that – but suddenly I felt that maybe I'd discovered exactly the right career for me.

Mum patted my knee and smiled, without taking her eyes off the road.

"I think you'd make a lovely midwife," she said.

Karl called for me at seven o'clock. It was Friday evening, a week before Christmas, and I'd spent most of the time that I'd been home from school getting ready. Karl and I were going to the Young Farmers' Christmas Ball for the first time. Thomas had already been going for a few years and had always said he'd had a great time.

Dad went to the front door to let Karl in. I was in the living room, where Mum had just finished putting up my hair.

"Wow!" Karl said as he walked in. "You look nice."

"Thanks," I fingered the silk of my dress, "Monsoon sale; it was a quarter of the original price because one of the seams had split."

"You're looking very smart yourself," Mum said to Karl. It's true, he was: his dad had bought him a proper dinner jacket and everything because the Ball was going to be his first "black tie" event.

It was a cold night. Mum had lent me a black woollen wrap to wear over my dress. It was only a short walk from my house to the village hall where the Ball was being held, but Karl looked really cold without a proper coat. He just had his dinner jacket.

"You must be absolutely freezing," I said.

He smirked.

"Not quite absolutely," he said, "because as a matter of fact I'm wearing that belly button warmer that you gave me."

"Yeah right," I said.

"No, it's true actually," Karl said, and before I could stop him he'd pulled his shirt out of his trousers and undone a couple of buttons to reveal that he really had got this stupid little woolly thing in his belly button!

"Oh put it away!" I said, but I couldn't stop laughing. "I don't believe you sometimes, I really don't believe you!"

He grinned and tucked his shirt back in.

"Well, I wouldn't feel fully dressed on an occasion like tonight without my real sheepskin belly button warmer," he said, and put his arm round my shoulders as we walked the rest of the way to the hall.

The village hall had been transformed. It must have taken ages to put all the decorations up, and the caterers had laid out all these big round tables with proper white cloths, flowers and candles. Every place setting had two wine glasses, a carefully folded napkin and loads of cutlery for all the different courses. It looked fantastic. It seemed as if we were probably the youngest there, although Kirsty and Charlotte had said they were coming. We were offered champagne or orange juice as we arrived; I took the orange juice, but was glad that it was served in a champagne flute – the glass felt different and special in my hand.

Karl went off to find somewhere to put my wrap. While he was away I felt a dig in the ribs,

"Hi!" Kirsty said. "I like the dress."

"It's from Monsoon," I said, then looked at her and realised she was wearing the same dress, but in a different colour. "Hey, I really like yours too!" We both laughed.

The dress looked totally different on Kirsty. Whereas it was calf length on me, it fell almost to the floor on her.

"Come and see what Charlotte's wearing," Kirsty said, grabbing my wrist and dragging me across the hall. "Bit too much of a pink meringue for my taste, but she's somehow managing to look stunning in it!"

Charlotte's the only person I know who's actually a

member of the Young Farmers, and she was chatting to a few older lads at the bar.

"Well hello!" she said to me, then turned to her friends.

"This is Hannah," she said, and one or two of the lads nodded in my direction before resuming their conversation. Charlotte pulled me to one side.

"I must say," she said, "your date for the evening is looking rather gorgeous, isn't he?"

"My date...?" I said. "Oh, you mean Karl. Yeah, I suppose he does look quite good – I think all the blokes do when they're wearing a tux, don't they?"

Charlotte snorted, "If you say so, Miss French, but I would say – looking at your Karl this evening – that it's not surprising most of the lower school fancy him, and half the girls in *our* year come to that."

Everyone sat down at the round tables for the first part of the evening, and we were served a formal dinner. The food was something else, and I had to be careful that I didn't eat too much to enjoy the dancing. I let the wine waiter pour me one glass of white wine, but after that I switched to water, as I'd agreed with Mum and Dad.

After the meal some of the tables were cleared away to make room for a dance floor. The DJ was excellent, playing a good mixture of up to date music and old 70s and 80s disco stuff. Karl doesn't really appreciate disco or rave music but for once he seemed to be enjoying himself dancing, and even joined in the actions of 'YMCA' for probably the first time in his life.

The whole evening had been really great, and as we

left the hall afterwards the ground was so white with frost it almost looked as if it had been snowing. Our breath made clouds in the cold air as people shouted goodnight to each other. I put my arm through Karl's and snuggled into him to try and keep warm.

My teeth were chattering but otherwise we walked quietly. I was thinking about how it had been one of the best evenings I'd ever had. We were about halfway home when Karl stopped walking suddenly.

"What is it?" I said. He was staring into the night sky. He didn't say anything, but when I looked up I realised the stars were really bright and there somehow seemed to be more of them than usual.

I took a deep breath of the frosty air and tried to savour the moment. Then there was a split second when I was suddenly aware of Karl's face in front of my eyes before his cold lips made contact with mine. At the same time he grabbed me in a kind of bear hug, so that it was hard to breathe.

I pushed him away.

"What are you *doing*?" I demanded, wiping my hand roughly across my mouth.

Karl shoved his hands into his pockets. He was silent, and even in the moonlight I could see that he looked upset.

"What did you think you were doing?" I asked him again, but slightly more gently this time.

Karl shrugged and kicked his feet against the frozen verge.

"I wanted to ask you out," he said. "I didn't know how, I've been trying to ask you for ages."

I stared at him, open-mouthed.

"So," he said, "will you go out with me?"

"I think I'd just like to go home now," I said. And, turning away from him, I started walking.

I walked the rest of the way home as fast as I could. I hate being on my own in the dark and it was really late.

Mum had waited up for me, and was expecting to hear all about what a wonderful evening I'd had. I just told her that I was really tired and then went straight upstairs to have a shower and go to bed.

I took my dress off and let the silk fall in a heap in the corner of the bathroom. I didn't feel gorgeous like I had when I left the house earlier in the evening. I felt smoky and sweaty and confused. When I took all the pins out of my hair that Mum had used to put it up, it fell in heavy ridges, still held by the mousse and hairspray. My scalp felt really itchy. Stepping gratefully under the shower I lathered my hair twice, and soaped myself all over with raspberry shower gel. Then I just stood under the hot water, letting its comforting familiarity wash over me. I must have been in there quite a while when Dad knocked quietly on the bathroom door.

"Hannah, are you all right in there?" he asked, through the wood of the door.

"I'm fine," I said. "I'll be out in a minute."

I wasn't really fine, though. I lay in bed trying to think.

I knew I was closer to Karl than anyone. I knew he was really good-looking. And musical. And sporty. And generally talented. I knew loads of girls fancied him.

I grinned in spite of myself – it was quite flattering really. Gangly Hannah French, who's never had a boyfriend, gets asked out by the school heart-throb. Maybe I *should* go out with him?

But straight away I felt something twist inside me. I didn't want to go out with him. Karl was my friend, my best friend. I'd never wanted him to be my boyfriend.

But what if nobody else as nice ever asked me out again?

Deep down, though, I knew that I just didn't fancy Karl, whatever I tried to tell myself. And deep down I felt that I probably never would.

I buried my head in my pillow. I wished I could wake up and everything be back to normal. Too much was changing, first Mum getting pregnant, then finding out that the baby might be handicapped, all the different classes for GCSE, and now Karl wrecking our friendship by asking me out.

Then I realised that in less than a year Thomas would have left home. My swotty big brother would have gone to university. And for some reason that made me cry. I sobbed into my pillow until it was soaking wet, and eventually I think I must have cried myself to sleep.

The next morning I decided to go for a walk to clear my head. The ground was still white with frost as I headed down the path between the fields. I found myself making for the old lime tree and, slipping a bit on the icy wood, I climbed up into the natural tree house in the middle of it.

Dead leaves still covered the floor of the tree house, but it was midwinter now and the bare branches offered little protection against the biting wind. I must have lasted all of about two minutes before I felt so totally chilled that I eased myself back out down the tunnel and onto the ground. As I did so I remembered the last time I'd climbed out of that tree – when it had been summer and Karl had come to find me.

The rest of the weekend was fairly miserable. I had nothing to do except homework and wrapping Christmas presents, and I couldn't face doing either. I wondered if I should ring Karl, but I just didn't know what to say. I'd obviously made it pretty clear I wasn't interested, but I thought I had probably hurt his feelings too.

I was sorry if I had hurt Karl, but I was also quite angry with him: for ruining a perfect evening as well as changing the whole basis of our friendship.

As the weekend wore on, though, I gradually started to see things more from Karl's point of view. I realised that I had ruined his perfect evening as well as him ruining mine. But I also became more and more sure that I couldn't change how I felt. However good a catch Karl might be in terms of boyfriend material, I was sure he wasn't Mr Right for me. I tried to imagine snogging him, but the thought of it just made me squirm; the memory of that brief kiss he had given me was bad enough.

I'd quite often wondered what it would be like to have a boyfriend. There were one or two lads at school that I fancied a bit, but I'd never imagined *Karl* as my boyfriend. He was my friend; he was always there; he *had* always been there; he was almost family really.

As the hours ticked by on Sunday I started to dread Monday morning more and more. What was I going to say to Karl? What would it be like seeing him at the bus stop when the last time we'd met I'd stopped him kissing me? I knew loads of people would probably ask about the Ball; Nicola for one was going to want to know all the details, and I really didn't feel like talking about any of it – not even the good bits – any more.

Finally, on Sunday evening, Karl came round to the house. I hadn't told my family much, but they'd rumbled the fact that something had happened between me and Karl, and when he arrived they all managed to discreetly disappear.

"I suppose you'd better come in," I said. I took him into the living room. Somehow my bedroom didn't seem an appropriate place to speak to him now.

Dad had just stoked up the fire and so it was roaring away in the hearth. I curled myself into a ball in one of the armchairs and stared into the flames, not looking at Karl.

It seemed like several minutes passed without either of us saying anything. Karl hadn't sat down, he just stood in the middle of the room shifting awkwardly from one foot to the other.

Finally he spoke.

"Hannah?" He pulled on his fingers, cracking the joints one by one. "Look, I'm sorry and everything, but I need to know how you feel."

"I thought that would have been obvious," I said. I turned my head and forced myself to look into his eyes. I wanted to make sure he got the message. "I don't want to go out with you, Karl."

"I know," he looked away from me, "I didn't mean that. I mean can we go back to how things were? Can we still be friends and everything?"

"Sure," I said, and looked back into the fire.

He stood there for a while longer. I couldn't think of anything else to say.

"Right then," he said at last, "I'd better go. See you tomorrow?"

I nodded without looking up; it was all so embarrassing. I heard him let himself out of the front door.

On Monday morning I made sure I got to the bus stop as late as I could without missing the bus. Karl arrived about the same time. We said "hi" to each other but then stood a way apart, both watching the road intently for the bus to arrive. I saw Thomas looking from me to Karl and back again in a curious sort of a way, but was grateful that for once he had the tact not to say anything.

I got onto the bus first and sat in our usual seat near the front. I took the window seat and put my bag on my lap so Karl had the choice of whether or not to sit down. I stared out of the window so that I wouldn't catch his eye, but he walked straight past and must've sat somewhere further up towards the back.

I realised that I was glad that after tutor group I wouldn't have to see him again for the rest of the day. It was horrible to think that our friendship had come to that.

Chapter 6

As long as I live, I will never forget today.

I woke up at five o'clock this morning to the sound of the front door closing. I could hear Dad talking to someone downstairs, and realised it must be the midwife. Mum must be in labour, I thought, swinging my legs over the side of the bed. Suddenly I had a really excited feeling in my stomach, thinking that our family would soon have a brand new baby!

I sat on the side of the bed for a minute, not knowing exactly what to do. I knew Dad didn't want us to get in the way. I heard steps on the stairs and a knock on my parents' bedroom door, then a click as it opened and shut. I could hear the midwife talking quietly to my mum. I strained to hear what was being said.

"Hello again, Yvonne. What's been happening?"

"Hi, Claire, I'm glad it's you on duty." My mum's voice didn't sound quite normal, sort of how it goes when she's really tired or a bit upset. "I've been having pains since one o'clock, and they're coming quite close together now."

"OK then, I think I'd better examine you now and see how you're getting on; let me know if there's a contraction coming and I'll have a listen to the baby's heart."

That could be me in a few years' time, I thought; driving around in the dead of night to deliver babies. Everything I'd seen of the midwives' work while Mum had been pregnant seemed interesting, but this part – the actual birthing of babies – would be really mega.

Dad must have stayed downstairs. I decided to get up, and quickly pulled on jeans and a jumper before going down. I found Dad in the kitchen boiling the kettle.

"Hello love," he said turning towards me, "did we wake you?"

"It's OK," I said, "is Mum in labour then?"

"Seems so," he said, "although things don't seem to be happening as fast as they did with you. I'm making tea, do you want one?"

"Please." I watched Dad get two mugs and dunk the tea bags in them before adding the milk; he never bothers with the teapot.

We sat quietly sipping the hot liquid at the kitchen table, not saying anything. I could hear the midwife walking around upstairs. I yawned and wondered about going to wash my face.

I'd just drained my mug when we heard footsteps on the stairs and Claire, the midwife, came into the room.

"Hello, Hannah," she said. I was dead impressed she'd remembered my name, when she must meet so many people. She turned to my dad. "Yvonne's asking for you, Tony, and says please will you bring her a cup of tea."

"I'll get it," I said straight away, glad to have something I could do. I got a tray out as they went back upstairs. I put a pot of tea on it with a jug of milk and two cups – one for the midwife. I added a bowl of sugar just in case and carried it carefully upstairs. I tried to balance it to knock on the bedroom door, but in the end had to put it down. It felt really weird to have to knock, as usually I just wander into Mum and Dad's room – it's them that have to knock to come into mine.

Dad opened the door and told me to come in. I wasn't sure what to expect, but Mum was just sitting up in bed wearing a big T-shirt with her hair scraped back into a ponytail.

"Hello darling," she said smiling at me, and patted the bed beside her, "come and sit with me for a bit."

I put the tray down on the dressing table and poured her a cup of tea; I handed it to her then sat down on the side of the bed. It was strange because she's my mum and everything, but I suddenly felt really shy and didn't know what to say to her.

She hugged me with one arm, holding the tea in her other hand. "Are you excited?" she asked me.

"Yes," I said, turning to look her in the face, "are you?"

She nodded, smiling, and gave me a squeeze. Then I felt her grip tighten, and she grimaced, gesturing to Dad to come over, and passing the tea back to me. She turned to Dad, grabbing his hand with both of hers, and rocked backwards and forwards lying on her side. Claire came over and put one hand on Mum's tummy while she looked at her watch. It seemed ages before Mum relaxed and turned back over.

"Whew," she said and managed to smile as she took the tea back and had a few sips.

"They're lasting about a minute now," Claire told her. Mum nodded and raised her eyebrows.

"How long is it going to be before the baby comes?" I asked. Mum looked across at Dad before she answered me.

"Claire's examined me and had a feel of the baby," she said, "and it seems that the baby isn't in quite the right position at the moment." She must have seen me look anxious because she took my hand and said, "Everything else seems to be okay, and the baby's heartbeat is still fine, so Claire says we'll wait a bit and see what happens. Why don't we pray about it?"

I nodded and the midwife slipped out of the room saying she was just going to wash her hands. Mum finished her tea, then she, Dad and I all held hands, sitting on the bed, and Dad started to pray.

"Dear Lord, we ask your protection on Yvonne, and on our child. Please give them both strength at this time, that all may be well and our baby born safely. May your will be done, in Jesus' name, Amen."

Just as Dad said "Amen", Mum's grip tightened again, and when I opened my eyes I could see she was having another pain.

"Shall I get the midwife?" I asked and Dad nodded. I eased Mum's hand from mine and passed it over to Dad. Just as I was leaving the room I met Claire coming in anyway. I wished that Karl and I were still friends; I would have liked to have phoned him and told him what was happening. I really missed having someone of my own age I could talk to about anything at any time.

I decided it was time to tell Thomas what was happening. As I went into his room I could have done with a clothes peg because it has that horrible teenage boy's smell, especially when he's asleep in it, which he was, huddled under his navy blue duvet. It's a family joke that if anyone could sleep through a bomb falling Thomas would! I shook him gently.

"Urgh, go away," he mumbled, "what time is it?"

I switched the light on to look at the clock on his bedside table, and was surprised to find it already said half past six. Thomas pulled the duvet over his head to block out the light.

"What did you do that for?" he whinged.

"To look at the clock, stupid," I said. "It's half past six in the morning, but Mum's in labour, I thought you'd like to know."

"Is she okay?" he asked, struggling out from under the duvet and sitting up, rubbing one eye.

"Yeah," I nodded, "but there's something about the baby not being in the right position or something."

"What position is it in?" he asked.

"I don't really know," I said. "They said they're going to wait a bit and see what happens." Then the two of us just sat there talking for a while about things we'd done when we were kids, family holidays we'd had just the four of us and stuff. After a while I didn't notice the smell in his room anymore. Every so often we could hear low moans from the room next door, and just kind of looked at each other, but it was nice sitting there like that together, we hadn't talked so much for ages. I put on *Pachelbel's Canon* on Thomas' CD player; it's probably my favourite piece of classical music. Then I went over and opened his curtains and it was getting light, with a big red sun coming up over the fields opposite. I think the beauty of that moment, along with the music, and the excitement I was feeling about the baby coming, will stay with me always.

Suddenly things started to happen. Dad came in and told us that Claire said Mum needed to go to hospital because she wasn't making any progress. I could hear Mum crying and saying that she wanted to go home, over and over again, which didn't make much sense really as she was still at home.

"Can I see Mum?" I asked Dad, and he looked a bit doubtful for a second then agreed.

"OK then, but you'll have to be quick because Claire's already gone downstairs to phone for the ambulance," he said.

I went into the room next door and was really shocked by how different Mum looked now. She stopped moaning when she saw me and tried to smile, but her eyes looked really wild. I noticed the bed was all crumpled and I could see what looked like a bit of blood in places.

"Are you all right, Mum?" I asked her.

She nodded but started crying again.

"I just want my baby now," she said.

I grabbed her hand and squeezed it really hard. I turned to Dad.

"Are you going in the ambulance with Mum?" I asked.

"I wish I could, but I don't think I can," he said. "I think I'll take the car so I can get home again afterwards." He looked a bit uncomfortable.

"I'm going to come with you then," I said, turning back to Mum, "and Thomas can go with Dad." I could see Dad was going to protest about me going, but Mum thanked me and just about managed another smile, so he didn't.

In the ambulance Mum was on a stretcher and I was strapped in on a sideways facing seat that made me feel a bit sick. Claire and one of the paramedics came in the back of the ambulance as well. As we reached the outskirts of town the paramedic who was driving turned round and told us he was going to put the blue lights and siren on because of the heavy rush hour traffic. I have to admit that was pretty exciting even though I was feeling so awful for Mum – I'd never been in an ambulance before.

When we got to the hospital I stayed with Mum, holding her hand, as they wheeled her along a corridor and into a delivery room. They put her onto the bed, and then Dad arrived and told me I was to go and find Thomas in the waiting area.

It was a bit of an anticlimax to be stuck in the waiting room with nothing I could do to help. We couldn't even hear what was going on any more. I walked around a bit and looked at the vending machines, but neither of us had any money with us.

I started looking at the posters on the walls; one of them advertised breastfeeding as "free fast food for babies". Thomas was flicking through some magazine he'd picked up, but I could tell he wasn't really concentrating on it.

After a while I sat down again and Thomas put down the magazine. All I could think about was what Mum might be going through.

It seemed to be ages that we sat there like that, not

saying much, just waiting for some news. I was praying inside my head a bit, asking that Mum would be all right and not have too much pain.

Eventually Dad came out to see us. He looked really upset. I told him to sit down and went over to get him a cup of chilled water from a free machine that Thomas and I had discovered. I gave it to him and asked what was happening.

"Your mum's all right," he said, but I could see him shaking as he held the water in both hands, "I want you to know that, they say she's going to be all right."

"What about the baby?" I asked, suddenly feeling fear claw at my stomach. I hadn't been praying for the baby. I'd assumed the baby would be all right. Dad bit at his top lip before he answered.

"They say the baby's showing signs of distress," he said and put his face down into his hands, so I could only just make out what he said next.

"Its heart has slowed right down. They're taking your mum now to have a Caesarean."

"Aren't you going with her then?" Thomas demanded.

"I can't," Dad said, "I just can't," and actually started to cry. I'd never seen Dad cry before. Thomas and I looked at each other. We knew he was right, he'd probably pass out or something if he had to go into the theatre with Mum.

"Right then, I'm going to go with Mum," I said. "You look after Dad, Thomas," and I dived back into the delivery suite before either of them could argue. I was really nervous about what I was doing and also, I suddenly realised, really frightened for the baby, as well as Mum.

"God," I prayed, "you know we were all really shocked about having this baby to begin with. If I'm honest in some ways we didn't even really want it, but we do now so please, please, let it be all right."

It was true; even though we hadn't met the baby yet it was already part of our family. If anything happened to it now there would always be a part of us that was missing: my little brother or sister.

"Please let the baby be all right," I prayed again, "even if it's handicapped or anything, we still really want it."

I caught up with Mum as she was being wheeled towards theatre and told her I was coming with her. For once my height was a real bonus, because nobody bothered to check how old I was. Well it was either that or they were all too busy with what was happening to care. Claire told me I'd have to change into theatre "blues", and quickly took me into a changing room where she gave me a pair of what looked like baggy cotton pyjamas. When I'd changed into them she took me into the theatre and got me a stool to sit on next to Mum's head. Mum was lying flat on her back in the middle of the room, while everyone else was charging around her getting ready for the operation. All the time I was praying in my head, just asking God to make everything all right.

"How are you?" I asked Mum as I took her hand again. "Is it still really painful?"

"No," she said, "they've given me an epidural for the operation, so the pain's gone. I'm just worried for the baby; are you praying?"

I nodded. I was really impressed by how brave she was; after I'd had my appendix out Mum told me she was really proud of me, because she would hate to have an operation. And now here she was about to have one fully conscious, but all she cared about was the baby.

They put a big green sheet up as a screen just below Mum's neck, so we couldn't see the gory bits of what was going on. It all happened really quickly, and it only seemed like a couple of minutes before someone said "It's a boy" and briefly lifted a little curled up purple baby above the screen for Mum to see before rushing him off to a trolley thing in the corner.

"Is he all right?" Mum wanted to know. "Is my baby alive?"

"He certainly is," Claire said, coming over. "The doctor's just going to give him some suction and oxygen and then you'll be able to hold him."

A few minutes later she wrapped the baby up in a white blanket with just his face showing and brought him over to Mum, who was still lying flat on her back. Mum put out her hand and pulled the blanket away from his face a bit more.

"Oh," she said, "he's absolutely gorgeous! Isn't he lovely, Hannah?"

I nodded, although actually his face was all sort of crumpled and still had some blood on it. Mum managed to twist her head round and kiss the baby; then she pulled my head down to her and kissed me too.

"Well," Claire said, "he is lovely, but I'll have to tear myself away to fill in some paperwork. Would big sister like to hold him while Mum's being stitched?"

She gently handed me the surprisingly heavy little bundle, and I held my little brother in my arms for the first time. I can't really begin to describe what that felt like. It really was all just such an amazing miracle. A few minutes before he had been part of my mum, and now he was his own little person – looking more human by the second.

I suddenly realised there was something I still needed to know, and called Claire back.

"It doesn't matter," I said, "we love him anyway, but has he…" I hesitated, glancing at Mum who was looking at me questioningly, "*has* he got Down's syndrome?" I blurted out.

Claire smiled at me, "No," she said, "no – I should have said – no, he hasn't."

I looked at Mum and she was looking lovingly at me and the baby. She put her hand on my arm, so it was touching him as well, and I realised that she and I were both crying. Tears of joy.

I looked back down at my little brother and to my delight he yawned and then slowly opened his eyes for the first time. He blinked at the bright lights before fixing me with his gaze.

"Welcome to the world, little one," I said.

Chapter 7

My baby brother weighed in at 7lb 6oz. Mum and Dad named him Benjamin James, but soon everyone was calling him "Benji".

It was five days before we were able to take him home, because Mum had to stay in hospital after having the Caesarean. Benji seemed to have spent most of the time in hospital asleep, but when he came home he was suddenly much more alert, looking around him and staring in apparent fascination at blank walls and ceilings.

When I was little I had never been into playing with dolls like other girls – I couldn't stand the fact that they weren't real! Now I had the chance to make up for it, and I was absolutely loving it. Because of Mum's Caesarean there were certain things she wasn't supposed to do, like lifting and housework. I used it as an excuse for virtually taking over the care of Benji. I changed him, washed him, pushed him round the village in his pram, rocked him to sleep... When I had been visiting in hospital I had even been the one who gave him his first bath, under the supervision of one of the auxiliary nurses. The only thing I couldn't do was feed him, because Mum was breastfeeding. Unfortunately the flip side of all this was that while

Mum was recovering I was also expected to do all the hoovering, half the washing-up, and keep the bathroom clean. Dad did the other half of the washing-up and most of the cooking. Thomas somehow managed to wheedle his way out of doing anything by muttering something about A levels.

I tried not to mind too much – I hate doing housework, but I was still feeling quite protective of Mum, so most of the time I just got on with it when I had to.

School was fast becoming an irritation because it was taking me away from "my" baby. I couldn't get home fast enough to see him at the end of the day. I started to let my work – especially homework – slide a bit. It just wasn't my most immediate priority, and I reassured myself that I would catch up later.

We had *so* many visitors. Everyone from church, family, friends, teachers from school who'd got to know Mum, and most of the women in our village. They almost all brought some sort of present for the baby: little outfits from Mothercare, toys from the younger people, knitted hats and bootees from the older ladies... After each visitor left, Mum took a little card from the stack she'd got in and wrote a thank you note. Even at school, girls from Years 7 and 8 were coming up to me in the corridor with little gifts and asking if I could please give them to Mrs French. They mostly seemed to be bibs and little spoons or feeding bottles, none of which Benji needed yet! But Mum thought it was really sweet of them – she reckoned they must be using their pocket money to buy them – and would send me back to school the next day with one of her thank you cards. I was starting to feel like a carrier pigeon, and to be quite honest, tracking down people at school who I don't even know is not my ideal way to spend time.

One present that I did appreciate arrived the first weekend that Mum and Benji were home from the hospital. Karl called round bringing a baby-gym that he said was from his mum. I knew it wasn't. The gym was the exact same one that had caught my eye one time when Karl and I had been in town together a few months ago. It was carefully wrapped up in "It's a Boy!" wrapping paper, and the matching gift tag – signed in his mum's name – was in Karl's handwriting.

I was glad that he'd come round, because I really wanted to introduce him to Benji. Karl dutifully peered into the Moses basket to admire him, and even smiled a bit when Benji gurgled in his direction, but the atmosphere between us was still really awkward. I don't know whether it helped or not that Mum was in the room all the time he was there.

He only stayed about ten minutes. When he had gone I turned to Mum.

"Don't you like the gym?" I asked her.

"Yes, of course," she said, "it's a very nice baby-gym. Why?"

"Oh, nothing really. It's just that you'd usually have started your thank you note by now."

"I see," Mum smiled. "But I think this is one thank you note *you* could manage to write," she said, handing me one of her little cards in a meaningful sort of a way.

Writing that card posed me a bit of a problem. How could I write and thank Mrs Lennox for a present which she quite likely knew nothing about? On the other hand I couldn't exactly address it to Karl – it would almost amount to calling him a liar! In the end I wrote the card as if it was to his mum, but handed it to Karl at the bus stop, asking him to give it to her for me.

Thomas was trying to make out that he thought all babies, Benji included, were a dead loss.

"It's not like he even knows we're here," he said, "he just wees and poos and eats and sleeps. I'm glad I don't have to look after him."

Actually, though, it was obvious that Thomas loved Benji as much as the rest of us did. He'd sit on the sofa watching TV in the evening with Benji lying alongside him. And often if I looked over I'd see that Benji had his little hand curled tightly round one of Thomas' fingers. One thing I didn't get though, was how come Thomas had time to watch TV but not to help around the house?

Thomas also insisted on trekking all of his mates into the house to meet Benji. You could tell all these seventeen and eighteen year old lads weren't really interested in meeting a baby. It was ironic really, because they'd be pretending to admire Benji, and making polite comments about him to Mum, while Thomas would be standing there saying, "See, I told you he's a waste of space, didn't I?"

When Benji was ten days old we took him to church for the first time. All five of us went together, with me pushing the pram. Our village church is an old stone building that was built hundreds of years ago. Despite the heaters it never gets warm in winter, so some people might've said that it was not a very brilliant idea to take a new baby there in January. But in actual fact I think Benji was probably the only person in church that morning who wasn't cold. He was tucked up in his pram with hat, mittens, bootees and several blankets, including a fleece. I was sitting at the end of the pew, next to the pram, and Mum kept nudging me because she wanted me to put my hand on his cheek to check he wasn't getting too hot!

I don't remember a lot about the service – watching Benji was too much of a distraction. But one of the readings was from Psalm 139. I was sitting there not really paying much attention while Mrs Simms was reading, when I suddenly became aware that it was about God making babies, creating life unseen within the mother's body. The words were really moving, especially when I looked down at Benji snuggled up in his pram beside me.

When the other readings had finished the organist played a few bars of music while Rev Alder made his way to the pulpit and then we all sat down. I don't generally listen to the sermon; quite often I secretly read the notice sheet or something. This week was no exception – I reached out and picked up the pew Bible from in front of me. I ploughed my way through the pages, as quietly as I could, until I found the psalm that had been read out. What I was looking for was in verses 13 to 16:

For you created my inmost being;
you knit me together in my mother's womb.
I praise you because I am fearfully and
   wonderfully made...

My frame was not hidden from you
when I was made in the secret place.
When I was woven together in the depths of the
   earth,
your eyes saw my unformed body.
All the days ordained for me were written in your
   book
before one of them came to be.

I don't know whether I'd never read that psalm before, or if it just meant more since Benji. I thought about how we'd seen Benji that one time on the ultrasound pictures, and then imagined how God must have been able to see him all the time that he was growing inside Mum. I'd already decided that Benji was a complete miracle, the way he had come from not being anyone at all this time last year to being such an amazing little person now. But somehow this psalm made it all much more personal. It wasn't just Benji whose creation was so incredible, it was mine as well. It made me feel very safe and loved somehow, to think that long before I could remember – before Mum even knew she was pregnant with me – God knew all the person I would ever be.

Chapter 8

Benji was crying again.

He was in Mum and Dad's room, but it was the third time he'd woken me that night.

I stumbled out of bed and across the landing to the bathroom, only to find that the door was locked.

It was the middle of the night and the house was freezing cold. I stood outside the bathroom door and shivered, with my eyes closed, trying not to wake up too much. The toilet flushed at last, and I heard the tap running. Then the door was unlocked and Thomas emerged. The sudden light that flooded out as he opened the door hurt my eyes.

"Blooming baby," he said.

I grunted a bad-tempered response, and pulled off the light as I went into the bathroom. All I could think about was getting back into bed as quickly as possible and going back to sleep. Benji had stopped crying – Mum was probably feeding him.

I crawled back under my duvet. The bed was cold now and I curled up as tight as I could, trying to get warm.

I couldn't get back to sleep.

The more I thought about how tired I was, and what a wonderfully deep sleep I had been in before Benji had woken me, the more stressed I got.

The past week or so had been horrendous. Mum said that Benji was really good during the day. But come five o'clock each evening – just when I was home from school and changed, ready to have tea, do some homework and watch TV – he'd start crying. And then it seemed like he cried almost continuously until he fell asleep at about eleven o'clock. Dad and I took turns to walk around holding him, and every so often Mum would give him a feed, but nothing worked for long. As soon as he was asleep it was a mad scramble for the rest of us to get ready for bed and get our heads down, to try and get some sleep before he woke us all up again a few hours later. It was really starting to get me down.

Mum said Benji had "colic", and that it would pass by the time he was three months old. Apparently Thomas and I had both had it too. But it was another eight weeks until he'd be three months. I didn't think I could take another eight weeks of this.

At breakfast the next morning it emerged that neither could Thomas.

"I'm moving out," he announced, as he poured milk over the three Weetabix arranged in his bowl.

"What's that?" Mum said, yawning and rubbing her eyes as she filled the kettle at the sink. It seemed unfair that we all had to be up while Benji was still sleeping upstairs.

"I'm moving out," Thomas said again, as Dad came into the kitchen in his dressing gown.

"You're doing no such thing," Dad said, "so you can get that idea right out of your head straight away."

I looked from Dad to Thomas. I doubted that

Thomas would just leave it at that. I was right.

He stood up and slammed his spoon down into his cereal bowl, making the milk slosh over the side of the bowl onto the table. It had little soggy bits of Weetabix in it.

"So how am I supposed to work with that THING yelling all the time then?" Thomas shouted. "I didn't ask you to have another baby, and I don't see why it should be allowed to screw up my whole future!" He squared up to Dad, as if they were about to have a fight, but Dad isn't a very confrontational person.

"We're a family, Thomas," he said, "that means the good bits and the bad bits. We see them through together."

"Oh right," said Thomas, "so we all have to suffer do we? Excellent plan, I DON'T think."

"Thomas, please," Mum said, trying to get him to sit down again, "can't we talk about this later?"

"No," he said, "sorry Mum, but I've decided. My exams are only a matter of weeks away now, and it is just a complete joke trying to do any work round here. I'm moving out – I'm going to Dave's – and," he said, turning to Dad, "you can't stop me."

We had a whole school assembly that morning. We were lined up, waiting to go into the hall and I was telling Nicola about Benji's colic.

"No talking," Mrs Reed said.

I carried on in a whisper.

"Hannah, didn't you hear what I said?" Mrs Reed said. I shut up as we all filed into the hall and sat down on the floor behind Year 9.

There was a steady hum of whispered conversation,

interspersed by teachers telling us to be quiet and a creaking noise as the hall door was opened and closed. The sixth form wandered in, and I looked at them enviously as they sat down on the chairs which had been laid out for them. They didn't have to wear uniform either. I spotted Thomas laughing with one of his mates, and none of the teachers told him to shut up or anything.

I yawned.

At last Mr Gray, the deputy head, stood up.

"SILENCE!" he shouted.

Nearly everyone went quiet. Those who didn't got yanked off the floor by their form tutors and made to sit by the teachers' chairs.

"Let us pray," Mr Gray said.

I groaned inwardly. School prayers were awful. For one thing, you could hardly hear Mr Gray for all the sniggering that was going on under bowed heads; for another thing it was really annoying how these "prayers" were always about working hard at our lessons and getting good exam results for the school. And people were always looking at me to see what I was doing during prayers, because they knew I went to church. I didn't know whether to keep my eyes open to show that I didn't like this sort of prayers, or close them like I do when Rev Alder prays or when Mum or Dad say grace before meals.

At the end of the prayer everyone competed to see who could make their "Amen" last the longest, or get away with saying it in the stupidest voice.

It was a relief when it was all over and we could get on with the rest of the assembly. Mr Gray read out various notices about things like the school fête, and how many people had been offered university places this year.

"Could everyone involved in the cross country running competition please meet outside the changing rooms after school," he read from a piece of paper, "oh yes, and that reminds me – could Karl Lennox please come up here to the front?"

Karl?

All eyes in the hall seemed to be directed at our tutor-group, and I watched Karl unfold his crossed legs and stand up, before picking his way through the rows of people to get to the front of the hall.

"Karl," Mr Gray said, in the sort of friendly voice he usually reserves for other members of staff, "would you like to tell us all about your latest achievement?"

Anyone else would have been really embarrassed, but Karl has been out the front so many times for sporting achievements, national maths contests awards...

"Do you mean the orchestra?" he asked Mr Gray, who nodded.

Karl bent his head down close to the microphone and grinned as he addressed the assembled school.

"I've been accepted for the National Youth Orchestra," he said simply.

"That's right," Mr Gray said. "I'd like to publicly congratulate you, Karl, on successfully auditioning for the National Youth Orchestra, where I understand you'll be playing violin?"

Karl nodded.

I was hurt. Karl and I hadn't really been speaking, but we had seen each other every day on the bus and in tutor group. I'd have thought he could at least have told me about this himself, instead of letting me hear about it along with the whole of the rest of the school. Usually I would've known something like that within about five minutes of Karl himself knowing. He'd either have been round at my house or on the phone. We'd always told each other everything.

I felt cold inside, and sad. I wished we could be friends again.

Within twenty-four hours Thomas had indeed moved out to stay with Dave. It was just me left with Mum, Dad and the baby.

I still loved Benji, but he wasn't much fun any more. He screamed when I laid him down to change his nappy. He screamed when I got him out of the bath to dry him. He screamed when he wanted to be fed. He screamed all evening, especially if I dared to sit down when I had been walking around holding him.

To top it all I suddenly realised that I'd got four pieces of GCSE coursework due in the next few weeks.

"I don't know what I'm going to do, Mum," I told her. "I don't see how I can get them done when Benji's crying all the time."

Mum looked thoughtful.

"Hmm," she said, "I'll see what I can do."

A couple of hours later Mum called me to the phone.

"It's your Aunty Joyce," she said, "do you want to go out with her tomorrow evening?"

Aunty Joyce and I were sitting in Pizza Express looking at the menu. The waiter came over and we ordered a tomato and mozzarella salad and dough balls to start, followed by a pizza each and a salad to share.

I already knew Aunty Joyce was paying – she always does. She quite often gives me clothes as well. She's tall, like me, and says I might as well have her "hand-me-downs", but I think quite a lot of the time she actually buys me stuff specially. I don't feel bad, because Aunty Joyce isn't exactly strapped for cash: she's a doctor and although she's thirty-six she's not married or anything. She hasn't even got a big house to pay for, just a small flat in town.

"So," she said, "I hear you're thinking of midwifery as a career?"

"Yes," I said, "I went with Mum to some of her antenatal appointments and stuff and it all looked really interesting."

"You were at the birth as well, weren't you?" she asked.

"Well I was," I said, "but I didn't see much, I was just holding Mum's hand."

"Hmm," Aunty Joyce said, "so why midwifery, why not medicine?"

"Like you, you mean?" I said. "I don't know really. I've never wanted to be a doctor. I couldn't hack five years of medical school for starters."

Aunty Joyce laughed.

"Now speaking of starters..." she said, and sat back as the waiter approached our table with the salad and dough balls.

Later, as we debated whether we had room for dessert, Aunty Joyce asked if I'd enjoyed the evening.

"Yes," I said, "it's always great to see you and have a chat."

She smiled.

"And also," I said, feeling a bit guilty, "I've got to admit that it's really nice to get away from Benji for the evening. He's just been crying so much."

"Yes," Aunty Joyce said, "I heard about that. Your Mum says it's starting to affect your schoolwork?"

"It certainly is," I said, "I've got all this GCSE coursework I've got to do, but it's just impossible when he's crying so much. It's a complete nightmare."

"I should think it must be," she said. "I've been giving it some thought since your mum told me, and I wondered if you'd like to come and stay with me until the coursework's out of the way?"

I hesitated. There was nothing I'd like more. A chance to get my work done without distractions, and no awkward meetings with Karl on the bus – I could walk to school from the flat. But I remembered how Mum and Dad had reacted about Thomas moving out, and I didn't want to cause any more aggro. I looked down and fiddled with my napkin, trying to decide what to do for the best.

"I've already cleared the idea with your mum and dad, if that's what you're worried about," Joyce said.

"You have?" I said, looking up in surprise. I could feel a grin spreading across my face at the thought of a whole run of peaceful nights' sleep, without Benji crying. "Then thanks, I'd love to – that'd be great!"

Chapter 9

The flat was quite small, but luxurious.

Aunty Joyce used the smaller of the two bedrooms for herself and kept the larger room, with an en suite shower room, for guests. For the last eight days the guest had been me. So each night I'd had a double bed to stretch out in, and no baby crying! When Dad had driven me into town he had also brought our family's PC, which he'd set up for me on a little table in the corner of the room. So I was sorted really, except that there was no TV in the flat.

Because Aunty Joyce is a GP she was at work most evenings until seven-thirty or later. Most of the time I quite enjoyed letting myself into the empty flat and having the place to myself until she got home. As far as the coursework was concerned, it was excellent. I couldn't believe how much more I was getting done without any distractions. It was also good being able to do pretty much whatever I liked most of the time. But it did get a bit lonely at times.

For one thing it was weird not having my family around all the time. I was seeing Benji every few days – Mum had brought him to the flat, and Aunty Joyce had taken me home for a few hours on Sunday afternoon – but he seemed to have changed a little bit every time I saw him. He'd started to smile properly, and he was holding his head away from my shoulder for longer. I felt as if I was missing out on seeing all his little stages. I suppose I was missing him more because I was only seeing him in the afternoon – before he moved into screaming mode!

Going to church with Aunty Joyce was a bit of a culture shock. I knew she went to a big church in town, but I wasn't prepared for how packed it would be when we walked in on Sunday evening. We did manage to find two seats together – but only just.

I wriggled out of my jacket, trying not to nudge the man next to me, and hung it over the back of my seat. It was still a few minutes before the service was due to start, but a band had already been playing worship songs when we came in, and some people in the congregation were standing up and singing. I stayed sitting and looked around. There seemed to be an amazing number of young people – Thomas and I are the only young people in our church.

The worship band was excellent and I really enjoyed the songs, following on one after another. I was surprised that the service had already lasted over an hour when the minister got up to preach.

Usually I switch off during the sermon, but for some reason I found myself listening this time. Maybe it was just because it was someone other than Rev Alder preaching, or maybe it was because he somehow managed to make what he was saying quite entertaining.

He seemed quite young to be a minister, and he started off with this story about a horrible brown car he'd had when he first became a Christian. It kept breaking down on him and he was sure that it was because of this brown car that he couldn't get a girl-friend! He said he prayed every day that God would deliver him from his car. Anyway, one time when he'd got out of the car, while he was waiting for a ferry or something, he left it parked on a quayside. The next thing he knew a lorry had reversed into it and pushed it into the sea.

"So the Lord had answered my prayer," he said, "and in his infinite mercy he enabled me to buy a nice, shiny, *red* car with the insurance money! I'll have you know that that car hasn't broken down on me once in the five years I've had it. *And* I got a girlfriend." He grinned at one of the women in the worship band.

Aunty Joyce nudged me. "She's his wife now," she whispered.

The way the minister had told the story had had everyone creasing themselves laughing, and by the time he got onto the serious bit I found that I was actually quite interested in what he was saying.

"Can we be sure of our faith?" he asked. "Yes, we can."

"Amen!" the man sitting beside me said in a loud voice, making me jump.

"Amen indeed," the minister said, smiling in our direction. "Yes, we can be sure of our faith. And I'll tell you why."

He went on about how God can satisfy our minds as well as our hearts. I didn't really follow everything that he was saying at that point. And anyway, I thought, there isn't any real evidence to believe, is there? That's why a lot of clever people like Karl are atheists, isn't it?

I tried to put my thoughts to one side and get back to what the minister was saying. Throughout the sermon he'd been holding a Bible, which he kept waving around. Now he opened it.

"Let's take a look at some verses from God's word," he said. He gave out some Bible references, and people started picking up Bibles and flicking through them. A lot of the people sitting around me seemed to have brought their own Bibles with them, even though each seat had a church Bible in front of it.

The minister read out a couple of short passages. I got the general gist. It was about how God gives evidence of his existence through creation. Pretty much what I'd been trying to get over to Karl the day of our forty-mile bike ride.

"So that's my first point," he said. "God gives us a general revelation of his existence through creation. But then God reveals himself to us *personally*: through Jesus, the Bible, and his relationship with us in prayer".

He smiled.

"And it *is* a relationship, because God listens to our prayers and he answers them. Like what I was telling you earlier about my car – that's just a light-hearted example – but he really does answer us. Maybe not always in the way that we want, maybe not always at the time that we want, but according to his will and his perfect timing. We can rest assured in that knowledge – that he WILL answer prayer."

He paused for a minute, turning and nodding to the worship band, who were sitting on chairs on the platform. They started to get up and quietly pick up their instruments.

"I'd like you to be thinking about what I've said as

the band take us through this next song," he said, and went to sit down as the band's violinist started to play unaccompanied.

It was a beautiful tune that I didn't recognise, but the people around me obviously did, because during the first line of the song more and more people started singing quietly, some standing, some sitting. At last the overhead projector was switched on and the words flashed up:

Did you ever talk to God above?
Tell him that you need a friend to love,
Pray in Jesus' name, believing that
God answers prayer.

The words seemed incredibly relevant to me – I missed Karl's friendship so much. I suppose the fact that it was just the violin that was playing got to me as well, because of it being Karl's instrument. But whatever it was I found that I was close to tears by the time the keyboard, flute and other instruments gradually joined with the violin in the second verse.

OK then, God, I prayed silently, this is my prayer: that somehow you would put things right between me and Karl, so that we can go back to being proper friends again.

Then I remembered the prayers I'd said for Mum and "the baby" before Benji was born. I couldn't remember whether I'd ever actually got round to thanking God for answering them. So I sent him a quick "thank you" before I joined in to sing the third verse of the song.

* * *

Aunty Joyce made us both a coffee when we got back to the flat.

"Did you enjoy the service?" she asked, as she handed me my mug.

"Mmm, yeah," I said, as we carried our coffees through into the lounge. "I suppose it was a bit too long, but I thought the band was really good. And I got quite interested in what that minister was saying – although I don't understand how he can say some of that stuff."

"How do you mean?" Joyce said, putting her mug down on the dining table and sitting down. She put one of her elbows onto the table and rested her chin on her hand. At that moment I could just see her as "Dr French", sitting on the other side of her desk at the surgery, listening to hear what the 'patient' – me – had to say.

I tried to remember what she had just asked me, and not to laugh.

"Er," I said, "well, you know; about what he was saying about how there's evidence for faith. Well there isn't really, is there? I mean, I know he was saying about creation and prayer and stuff, but apart from that, there isn't any real evidence to believe, is there? That's why a lot of clever people are atheists, isn't it?" Like Karl, I thought, clever people like Karl.

Aunty Joyce raised her eyebrows.

"Well," she said, "I would've thought that creation and answered prayer should be enough to show us that God's real, but there's actually a lot of other evidence too." She got up and walked over to one of the bookcases, coming back with a paperback, which she handed to me.

"There you go," she said, "read that and I think you'll change your mind. If you're interested I've got other books I can show you, but that one'll give you a good starting point."

"Thanks," I said, not wanting to offend her; but inside I was wondering how she thought I had time to read books when the whole reason for me staying with her was so that I could get my coursework done.

On my last night in town I was really bored.

Amazingly I'd managed to get all the coursework done, and I'd even put it all into plastic folders ready to be given in. Whether or not it was any good, there wasn't really anything else I could do to it now.

Aunty Joyce had an evening surgery and was still out. I'd done myself a microwave lasagne, and had even made up a side salad to go with it. Now I couldn't think of anything else to do. What I really wanted was a television. I couldn't work out why Aunty Joyce didn't have one; she could certainly afford it. I glanced at the clock and realised that I was missing one of my favourite programmes. I wondered whether Mum or Dad would remember to video it for me. I thought of phoning them and asking if they could come and pick me up a day early, but decided that that wouldn't really be fair on Aunty Joyce, because she was expecting to see me when she got back from work.

It was definitely getting too late to go out into town on my own. I heaved a sigh of boredom and went for another wander round the flat.

Kitchen: solid wood units, trendy work surface, double oven.

Lounge: dining table, traditional leather suite, glass

fronted bookcases.

Bathroom: spotless white suite.

Aunty Joyce's room: bed made, Bible on bedside table.

My room, well the guest room really: bed unmade, bags packed as far as possible, some stuff still on floor... I wished Aunty Joyce would come home, I was *so* bored. The book she had given me to read was on the bedside table. I wandered over and picked it up.

I decided that I might as well glance through it, at least that way Aunty Joyce couldn't be offended that I hadn't bothered to read it.

I went back into the lounge and curled up in the corner of the sofa. I skimmed over the first few chapters. It seemed to have quite a lot of stuff in it, but it wasn't all that long. I decided to go back to the beginning and read it properly.

The book had lots of different sorts of evidence for Christianity in it. I started to wonder whether, if Karl read it, if it would make any difference to what he believed.

One of the longest chapters was about Jesus. It had a list of all these different prophecies in the Old Testament about God's Messiah. Then it showed how the prophecies had been fulfilled in Jesus, even though they were written ages before he was born. It gave the places in the Bible where you could find them, and I decided to go into Aunty Joyce's room to borrow her Bible and check some of them out. At times I needed to use the contents page at the front of the Bible, because I had a bit of trouble finding some of the passages.

I started off in the Old Testament, looking at Isaiah

chapter 40, verse 3. It said about someone in the desert preparing a way for the Lord. Then, when I flicked over to the New Testament and looked at Matthew chapter 3, I could see that Isaiah had been talking about how John the Baptist had got people ready for Jesus. I wondered whether other people bothered to look up the references when they were reading the book. Karl probably would, I thought. Although I wasn't sure if his family actually had any Bibles in their house.

I hadn't really spoken to Karl lately, but I still really cared about him. And I still hoped that God would answer my prayer and make us friends again.

I flipped through the Bible's thin pages to find another passage in the Old Testament, this time in Micah chapter 5, verse 2. It said that the "ruler over Israel" would come from Bethlehem. Wow! That had been written so many years before the Christmas story happened, but Jesus *had* been born in Bethlehem, even though his parents didn't live there!

After that I turned to Psalm 22. I recognised the first verse, because I remembered the story of the crucifixion. It was the words Jesus had spoken on the cross. And then, later in the psalm, it said "they have pierced my hands and my feet" – well, I could see that that was about Jesus being nailed to the cross – and "they divide my garments among them and cast lots for my clothing." I remembered that bit from the Easter story as well, so I didn't bother looking up Matthew 27:35–46.

I yawned, not because it wasn't interesting, but it was really tiring trying to concentrate. I got up and went through to the kitchen to pour myself a Coke from the bottle in the fridge.

Going back into the lounge, I got myself comfy on the sofa and put my Coke beside me, on one of Aunty Joyce's little tables. Then I had to flip through the book to find my place again. It said to look up Luke chapter 2, verses 25 to 33, where it had about this guy Simeon who'd been told he wouldn't die until he'd seen God's Messiah. And then when Mary and Joseph brought their baby to the Temple, Simeon knew that this was it – that Jesus was the Messiah.

The book also said that when Jesus came back to life, it wasn't just some holy Bible story, it was a historical fact. Now that was interesting! If Karl knew that, maybe he'd stop saying Christianity was all a load of rubbish. It gave the names of some really clever people who, like Karl, didn't believe it and had tried to disprove the resurrection; but then they ended up becoming Christians instead! Then the book asked a question – if Jesus wasn't God, who was he? I'd never thought about that before. It reckoned that, if he wasn't God, then he must have been either a liar or mad, because of the things he said about himself. And then it had another question – if Jesus didn't come back to life, why were his disciples prepared to die for claiming that he did?

Whew! It was all getting a bit heavy for me. But I knew I had to keep going because I had a feeling that these bits were just the sort of intellectual stuff that would appeal to Karl.

There was a chapter all about the disciples. It was amazing really, how they had left their jobs to follow Jesus just because he told them to. I'd never really thought much about that before either. I suppose it's because I've gone to church for as long as I can remember, that I just take the stories about Bible people for granted. The book said the disciples were so frightened when Jesus died, that they locked the doors when they met up together. But then Jesus rose from the dead. It said to look up John, chapter 20. This was turning out to be harder work than my coursework! But I looked it up anyway: it said about how the disciples couldn't find Jesus' body in his grave, and then Jesus suddenly appeared, and they knew it was him, and they knew he was alive – not just a ghost or an illusion or something. I could see what the book was getting at – it *was* amazing that the disciples were so sure they had seen Jesus alive, that they took terrible risks to tell people about him. Most of the disciples even ended up being killed for their faith in Jesus.

And then it got onto Paul. I shifted position slightly; my foot was going a bit numb. Paul wasn't one of the first disciples. In fact he was one of the people who were making life really difficult for the disciples after Jesus died and rose again. But then Jesus appeared to him too. The book said to look up Acts, chapter 9, but by that stage I'd had enough of looking stuff up, so I didn't. Anyway, then it said Paul spent the rest of his life telling people about Jesus, even though he was put in prison for it. The book said that there was an Oxford professor who tried to prove that Paul was never really a Christian at all. But after he had done a load of research about it the prof came to the opposite conclusion, and he ended up becoming a Christian as well!

There was a whole chapter about the Bible itself. It said about how it had been written by more than forty different people, over 1,500 years, in different countries, and in different languages; all of which meant that the Bible was totally different from any of the other books on my shelf.

I'd finished my Coke by this time. I thought about going to get another one, but I was nearly at the end of the book, so I decided to keep reading. It said how, for hundreds of years, people have been trying to ban the Bible and say it isn't true, and yet it's still the best selling book in the world and has been translated into more languages than any other book. One bit that really got to me was about this guy called Voltaire, who died in 1778. He reckoned that 100 years after his time Christianity would no longer exist. But in actual fact, fifty years after he died, a Bible Society took over the printing press in his house to produce Bibles!

Then I was onto the last chapter, and I was glad I'd kept reading, because this was the one that I liked the best. It was all about real people today, and what God had done in their lives. It showed how much difference Jesus could make to ordinary people. It made me glad that I'd grown up in a Christian family, where God had been real to me for as long as I could remember.

What was really annoying was that now I'd found all this evidence I wasn't actually able to show it to Karl. It was just the sort of thing he had often challenged me to produce, and laughed at me when I couldn't.

Aunty Joyce finally got in at quarter past eleven.

"Hannah, I am *so* sorry," she said as soon as she was in the door, "surgery ran really late and then I had house calls I had to make, and I ended up having to send two of them off to hospital... Have you eaten anything?"

"Yes," I said, "do you want me to get you anything?"

"No, that's OK, thanks, I'll just have a drink for the time being. Oh Hannah, I feel really bad – your last evening here and I've hardly seen you!"

"Don't worry about it," I shrugged, "it's not your fault, is it?"

I followed Aunty Joyce into the kitchen as she put the kettle on.

"Been busy?" she asked.

"Not really," I said, "pretty much everything's done now, I've just got to hand the coursework in. I've been reading that book you showed me."

"Oh?" Aunty Joyce put the coffee jar down and turned to look at me, "And?"

"It was really good, actually," I said. "I mean, don't get me wrong, I did find the intellectual stuff a bit heavy at times, but all the evidence it sets out – it's amazing! I don't know how I've managed to go to church all my life without knowing about these things."

Aunty Joyce smiled.

"I think you'd better keep the book," she said.

Chapter 10

It was three weeks since I'd been on the school bus and I nearly missed it.

Getting out of the house and down the road for ten past eight had come as a bit of a shock to the system. While I'd been staying with Aunty Joyce I could leave the flat at twenty to nine and still have plenty of time to get to school.

Today I'd actually had to run for the bus. I thought for a minute that I'd missed it, when I saw that it was already there as I came round the corner of the lane. In the end I got to it just as the driver was shutting the door. I climbed on, panting, and sat down.

"Whew," I said, as I started to get my breath back, "bit close for comfort that time."

Only then did I realise that I'd sat down next to Karl without thinking. He was sitting in our usual seat, and I'd plonked myself down beside him, forgetting that we weren't really speaking.

"Hi, Hannah," he said, and smiled.

I'd been looking forward to getting home from Aunty Joyce's in some ways, but I had also been a bit apprehensive. After having had several weeks of unbroken nights' sleep, I wasn't sure if I could cope with being woken every few hours by Benji again.

It was the day after I got home that I nearly missed the bus. I was woken by my alarm at seven-thirty. To start with I hit the "snooze" button, and then when it went off again eight minutes later I must have been a bit disorientated because I couldn't work out why I'd set it so early. Once I was properly awake, and realised I was at home, I couldn't believe Benji hadn't woken me once during the night!

I wandered downstairs in my dressing gown to get some breakfast. I was sitting drinking a cup of tea when Mum came into the kitchen with Benji.

"Hannah," she said, "what are you doing? Aren't you ready yet?"

"Hmm?" I said, then I looked up at the kitchen clock and saw that it was already a couple of minutes after eight! Talk about total panic – I had about three minutes maximum to get dressed and grab my stuff. Amazing that I caught the bus at all really.

I ended up sitting next to Karl on the way home from school too, but this time I was on the bus first and he came and sat down next to me. I'd sat down next to him accidentally in the morning, it had just been automatic, but I was glad that he had decided to sit with me again. Things definitely weren't back to normal between us though. We were sitting there having the sort of polite conversation that you have with elderly relatives at family gatherings.

"So you've got a place in the National Youth Orchestra?" I asked him.

"Yes," he said, "second violins for the time being."

"Oh well, congratulations," I said.

Silence. I was trying desperately to think of

something else to say. I realised I was fiddling with the straps on my bag, so then I acted like I was really fascinated in looking out of the window.

"I gather you've been staying with your aunt?" Karl said.

"Mmm," I said, turning my head back round, "that's right."

"Did you have a good time?"

"Yeah, it was all right," I said, "got my coursework done."

Karl nodded, "Excellent."

Pause. What should I say? Help! What should I say? I was fiddling with the straps again.

"I've been going to church with Joyce," I heard myself saying, "big church. Lots of young people, and they've got this really good band – well at least I thought they were good."

Karl didn't say anything, just raised his eyebrows slightly to acknowledge he was listening. Why had I said that? Religion wasn't his favourite topic at the best of times. What was I going to say now?

"My aunt – Joyce – gave me a really amazing book," I said. "You know how you're always getting at me to quote evidence for God and Christianity and stuff? Well this book's got loads of evidence in it."

"Such as?" Karl said.

"Lots of different stuff," I said. "I'll lend it to you."

"How come Benji's being so good then?" I asked Mum.

It was well into the evening and Mum and I were both sitting in the living room. Benji was awake but he was just lying quietly under his baby gym.

"He's been much better the last few days," Mum said. "Well, he is nearly three months old now, so hopefully that's the end of the evening colic."

"I didn't hear him last night either," I said.

"Oh, that's good," Mum said. "He did have a couple of feeds in the night actually, but I suppose he didn't really cry."

I bumped into Thomas at school a couple of days later.

"Heard you're back home?" he said.

"Yeah," I said, "It's all right actually."

"Really?" Thomas looked dubious, "What about the little resident loudmouth?"

"He's been OK since I got back," I said. "Mum reckons the worst is over now."

I don't know whether it was because of me saying that or whether Thomas had had enough of staying at Dave's anyway, but within a week he was back at home too. Mum and Dad seemed to have decided that they were going to act as if nothing had happened, because there was no more aggro about the fact that Thomas had moved out, or even about him just suddenly deciding he'd come back again.

Everything just seemed to go straight back to normal (well as normal as it could be with a new baby in the family). Mum and Dad had let me off the washing-up and stuff for the first couple of days I'd been back, but then I was expected to get on with it again. Thomas still seemed to be getting away with doing nothing – although I did notice he was spending more time in his room, and less in front of the TV, as his exams were getting closer.

I'd started to enjoy helping out with Benji again.

He really liked his baths, even chuckling as I lowered him into the water, and now that it was spring there was enough daylight for me to take him out in his pram after school as well as at the weekend.

Mum was busy writing out lists and invitations, because she and Dad had arranged that Benji was going to be baptised on Easter Sunday. Apparently this meant inviting practically everyone we know (including some relatives we haven't seen since my cousin's wedding three years ago) to the service and a buffet lunch afterwards.

"I suppose we *could* have kept it simple," Mum said, "but it's such a wonderful occasion – thanking God for Benji, and welcoming him into the church family – that I just want everyone to be able to share in that."

Dad lifted his head out of the gardening textbook he was reading, keeping one finger on the page.

"I couldn't agree more," he said to Mum, "although I don't know what you're planning to do with all these people if it rains."

"We'd better pray that it doesn't," said Mum.

Chapter 11

It was a late Easter. The daffodils were almost over, and as we walked to church I noticed that there were tulips out in some of the gardens that we passed.

Usually on Easter Sunday Mum and Dad go to eight o'clock communion and then come home for a family breakfast, with all our Easter eggs and stuff, before we all go together to the main family service. But this year, what with it being Benji's baptismal day and everything, neither of them got to the eight o'clock service. In fact as we scurried through the village with the pram, all five of us dressed in our smartest clothes, I thought we were probably going to be late for the eleven o'clock service.

We were OK, the organ was still playing quietly as we walked in – something classical – so I knew that the service hadn't started. For once the church was packed; all the pews filled with our family and friends. People shifted round in their seats to catch our eyes and wave. I spotted Aunty Joyce, Gran and Gramps, my cousins from Mum's side, Karl's parents... Karl's parents? I didn't know Mum had invited them, and they don't usually come to church. Karl wasn't with them and I found myself wishing that he was.

I wondered what Aunty Joyce thought about Mum

and Dad having Benji baptised. I knew that in her church it was adults that were baptised, not babies. At one of the services I'd been to with her, a baby had been dedicated to God. The parents had still made promises, saying that they would bring the baby up in the Christian faith, but he hadn't had any water poured on him. Aunty Joyce said that was so that he could be baptised when he was old enough to make the promises for himself.

I followed Mum, Dad and Thomas towards the front of the church. The organist finished the piece of music he had been playing and started another. I realised it was *Pachelbel's Canon*, my favourite. It was what Thomas and I had been listening to as the sun rose on the day Benji was born. About half a second after I recognised the music, I realised that it wasn't just being played by the organ, but also on violin. And the violinist was Karl!

Mum squeezed my arm.

"Surprise!" she said. "Karl said he'd like to play for the service as his way to congratulate us about Benji."

I sat down and listened to the music as the violin and organ accentuated and complemented each other, drawing out the haunting quality of the piece. I remembered our music teacher at school saying there was nothing worse than the violin played badly and nothing better than the violin played well. Just then Karl glanced up from the music, while he continued to play. His eyes locked with mine for a couple of seconds, and I found myself grinning at him with a lump in my throat.

Benji was baptised after the sermon, before the

communion. Rev Alder asked Thomas and me to come and stand by the font with Mum, Dad and Benji's godparents. I listened to the promises Mum and Dad were making for Benji: about turning to Christ, renouncing evil, and saying that they would pray for him, teach him the Christian faith and be an example for him to follow. It was quite moving to think of them making those same promises for me when *I* was a baby, and how they had kept them all through my childhood.

Rev Alder prayed that when Benji was older he would come to confirmation – to make the promises for himself which Mum, Dad and his godparents were making for him today. That made me think – I realised that I hadn't done that yet. I decided that I would speak to Rev Alder about it, and ask to be confirmed.

Then Mum passed Benji to Rev Alder, and he held him over the font while he gently poured the water over his head.

"Benjamin James," he said, "I baptise you in the name of the Father, and of the Son, and of the Holy Spirit."

Mum's prayers were answered: it was a fantastically warm spring day and the baptismal party spilled out of our house and into the garden.

I spotted Karl sitting with his parents on garden chairs under one of our apple trees. I was definitely glad we were speaking to each other again, although I thought that things were bound to be different between us. I went back into the house and helped myself to a glass of Coke and a mushroom vol-au-vent. It had been so nice to have Karl playing the violin in church.

I wondered what he had made of the service. He'd read the book Aunty Joyce gave me and said it was pretty interesting. I wondered if he'd been able to appreciate the Easter service now that he had some intellectual evidence for the resurrection.

I finished my Coke and decided to check on Benji. Mum had taken him upstairs for a feed and a nap when we'd got back from church. I pushed the bedroom door open as gently as I could, and peeked round it to look in the cot.

Benji was lying quietly, with his eyes wide open, looking around him.

"Hello, little brother," I said softly, walking over to the cot.

Benji turned towards me, giving me an enormous smile. I picked him up and he nuzzled his warm little head into my shoulder.

"It's your special day, Benji," I said, "we can't have you hiding away in here all the time." I took him over to the mirror and showed him his reflection; he smiled again and flapped his arms excitedly.

"Yes, you are a handsome boy, aren't you?" I said. "Come on then, let's go downstairs and meet your fan club."

It was probably the best Easter day I'd ever had, I thought, as I carried Benji around to be admired by all his adoring friends and relatives. I watched him looking at people and smiling, grasping the fingers they wiggled at him with his tiny, perfect, hands. I thought how much more relevant he seemed to the miracle of new life than the Easter eggs that we hadn't had time for at breakfast.

Of course everyone wanted to see Benji and most of them wanted to hold him. It was quite difficult in a way because I knew he'd get upset if he was passed around too much, but on the other hand it was his party and all these people had come specially to see him.

I decided to put him in his pram in the garden; that way everyone could carry on cooing over him, but he could relax a bit and look up at the trees.

I struggled to push the pram out of the back door with one hand, holding Benji in my other arm, but somehow it seemed to have got stuck.

"I wonder if I might be of any assistance at all?" It was Karl.

"That's a very formal choice of words," I teased him, grinning, "but yes please, I want to put the pram under those trees."

We walked across the lawn together, me carrying Benji, Karl pushing the pram. Dad had just announced that the buffet was served and most people seemed to be moving inside to feed their faces.

"That was really nice of you to play for the service," I said.

Karl looked a bit embarrassed and I saw him colour slightly.

"Yeah, whatever," he said, "I just wanted to congratulate you all on Benji and stuff. And I know *Pachelbel's Canon* is your favourite."

I laid Benji into the pram, straightening up his little white suit to make him more comfortable. Karl leaned over my shoulder, peering at him.

"What are you doing?" I asked him.

"Just looking at him," he said, "and wondering if maybe you're right after all. Because," he added, "all things considered, I don't think Benji looks much like a cosmic accident."

I laughed.

"You're daft," I said, "of course he's not." I pretended to punch Karl in the stomach and he pretended to be winded. That's when I realised that we were friends again, and said a silent thank you for yet another answered prayer.